WILD ANIMAL PLANET

How Animals Work

Series consultant: Michael Chinery

LORENZ BOOKS

This edition is published by Lorenz Books

Lorenz Books is an imprint of Anness Publishing Ltd
Hermes House, 88–89 Blackfriars Road, London SE1 8HA
tel. 020 7401 2077; fax 020 7633 9499
www.lorenzbooks.com; info@anness.com

© Anness Publishing Ltd 2002

This edition distributed in the UK by Aurum Press Ltd,
25 Bedford Avenue,
London WC1B 3AT;
tel. 020 7637 3225; fax 020 7580 2469

This edition distributed in the USA and Canada by National Book Network,
4720 Boston Way,
Lanham, MD 20706
tel. 301 459 3366; fax 301 459 1705; www.nbnbooks.com

This edition distributed in Australia by Pan Macmillan Australia,
Level 18, St Martins Tower,
31 Market St,
Sydney, NSW 2000
tel. 1300 135 113; fax 1300 135 103; customer.service@macmillan.com.au

This edition distributed in New Zealand by David Bateman Ltd,
30 Tarndale Grove, Off Bush Road, Albany, Auckland
tel. (09) 415 7664; fax (09) 415 8892

All rights reserved. No part of this publication may be reproduced, stored in a retrieval system, or transmitted in any way or by any means, electronic, mechanical, photocopying, recording or otherwise, without the prior written permission of the copyright holder.

A CIP catalogue record for this book is available from the British Library.

10 9 8 7 6 5 4 3 2 1

Publisher: Joanna Lorenz
Managing Editor: Linda Fraser
Editor: Sarah Uttridge
Production Controller: Claire Rae
Authors: Michael Bright, John Farndon, Dr Jen Green, Robin Kerrod, Rhonda Klevansky, Barbara Taylor
Illustrators: Julian Baker, Peter Bull, Vanessa Card, Stuart Carter, Linden Artists, Rob Sheffield, Sarah Smith, David Webb
Jacket Design: Alix Wood

PICTURE CREDITS

ABPL /Clem Haagner: 21c, 42-43c, 46b /M Harvey: 21tl. **Heather Angel**: 27bl, 39c. **Animals Animals**: 59tr. **ET Archive**: 37cl. The Bodleain Library: 35al. **BBC Natural History Unit** /Louis Gagnon: 49cr /Peter A Hinchliffe: 27br /Lockwood and Dattari: 33br /Alistair Macewen: 31cr /Klaus Nigge: 41bl /Anup Shah: 57bl /Doug Wechsler: 53cl. **Bridgeman Art Library**: 15b. **Adam Britton**: 23br. **Bruce Coleman**: 18bl / Erwin and Peggy Bauer: 38bl / RIM Campbell: 55tl /Janos Jurkai: 14br /Hans Reinhard: 51br /John Shaw: 43b. **Mary Evans Picture Library**: 13c, 20bl, 25b, 29bl, 40br. **FLPA**: 58t, 58bl /F Hartman:37br /Mark Newman: 40tr /Kim Taylor: 45t /Terry Whittaker: 34ar, 43tl, 47t. **Gallo Images**: 26tr. **Ronald Grant Archive**: 7tr. **Grant Museum** /A Lister: 45br. **Michael Holford**: 32bl, 46t. **Kit Houghton**: 28tr, 31br. **Innerspace Visions** /D Fleetham: 60tr /D Perrine: 60bl, 61bl /H Hall: 60cr. **Imagebank**: 38tr. **The Kobal Collection** /Ken Lucas: 36bl, 55cr. **NHPA**: 18tl, 19tr, 19bl / Michael Leach: 55br /Kevin Schafer: 13tr /M Wendler: 21tr. **Natural Science Museum**; 44b. **Nature Photographers**; 33ar, 59c. **Oxford Scientific Films**: 7tl, 7br, 9c, 9br Martyn Colbeck: 34bl Daniel J Cox: 39bl /David C Frith: 41br /David Haring: 53br /John R Jones: 35tr /Stan Osolinski: 22tr, 51tr /Andrew Plumptre: 55tr / E Robinson: 20tr / Gavin Thurston: 34al /Philip Tull: 29cr /Fred Whitehead: 29br /Konrad Wothe: 25tr. **Papilio Photographic**: 15t, 42t. **Planet Earth Pictures**: 59bl /P Atkinson: 61tr /Andre Baertschi: 57br /Darrock Donald: 24bl /Brian Kenny: 38br /D Mailland: 14t /K Lucas: 20-21, 51tl /Anup Shah: 54bl. **Premaphotos Wildlife** /K Preston-Mafham: 10tr.Ann Ronan: 37ar. **Science Photo Library** /Tim Davis: 52tr /Tony Stone: 42b. **Kim Taylor**: 6t, 7bl, 8, 10bl, 11ct, 25tl, 24-25m.**Visual Arts Library**: 17br, 58cr. **Volkswagen**: 9bl. **Warren Photographic**: 6b, 9t /Jane Burton: 14bl /Jan Taylor: 13tl /Kim Taylor: 11cb, 13tr, 13b

Contents

How Animals Work

Over a million different kinds or species of animals inhabit the Earth. They live on land and in the water and exhibit an amazing range of shapes and sizes, but they all have a number of things in common. They all move, feed, breathe, reproduce, grow, and get rid of waste. These features are characteristic of all living things, but the animals' bodies are constructed to carry them out in many different ways. You will discover how various animals live, and how their bodies are made to do the jobs necessary to keep them fit and healthy.

Polar bears can swim in the icy sea because they are protected by insulating fur and layers of thick fat.

Muscles for Movement

Animals can run, hop, crawl, fly, or swim, and these movements are all brought about by muscles. Each end of a muscle is firmly fixed to a part of the body and, when the muscle contracts, it makes something move. Among the vertebrates (animals with backbones)—most of the muscles are attached to bones. Contraction of the muscles at the top of a wolf's leg, for example, pulls on the bones lower down in the leg and lifts the leg up. Other muscles swing it forward and put it down again—the faster this happens, the faster the wolf runs. All vertebrates are built on a similar plan, but the shape, arrangement, and density of their bones vary. The skeleton of a bird's wing, for example, has the same basic structure as that of an ape's arm, but birds' bones, unlike mammals, are usually hollow. This makes them lighter, so flying is easier.

The muscles in the neck, shoulders, and hindquarters of wolves are very well developed. They give the wolf strength, stamina, and speed.

Invertebrate animals do not have bony skeletons, they have tough and sometimes very hard shells or cases (exoskeletons). Insects and spiders have lots of joints, rather like suits of armor. The joints are moved when they are pulled by muscles fixed to the insides of the armor.

Feeding

Food provides animals with energy and the materials needed for growth. Digestive juices break it down into simple substances that are absorbed into the body. Most animals specialize in either liquid or solid food.

Bugs and butterflies feed on liquids, such as plant sap and nectar, which they suck up through slender tubes. The drinking tubes of bugs have sharp tips that pierce the plants to reach the sap. Spiders feed on insects and other small animals, but they cannot eat solid matter, so they liquefy their prey with digestive juices before they swallow it. Beetles and many other insects have biting jaws and eat solid food, but their jaws are outside their mouths and they chew their food before pushing it into their mouths.

Most vertebrates have strong teeth, the shape and arrangement of which depend on the kind of food that is eaten. Cats and other carnivorous animals (meat-eaters) have sharp-edged teeth that slice through the meat. Baleen whales have no teeth: they filter small creatures from the water with the horny plates that hang from the roof of the mouth like drapes. Birds also lack teeth. Their horny beaks do the same job as teeth and, being lighter, they make it easier for the birds to fly.

Insects are protected by a hard outer layer called an exoskeleton which is waterproof and also prevents the insect from drying out in hot weather.

Breathing

Oxygen is necessary for life, and animals get oxygen from the air or water around them. Vertebrates that live on the land breathe with lungs. Air is drawn into these thin-walled pouches and the oxygen passes through the lung walls and into the blood vessels to be carried around the body. Fish breathe with gills. These are clusters of tiny, thin-walled fingers in the throat section. Water is taken in through the mouth and pumped over the gills, where the oxygen dissolved in it passes into the blood. The water then passes out through the gill slits. These slits are easily seen in sharks, but in most fish they are covered with a flap called an operculum. Insects' bodies have a number of tiny holes on each side. These holes are called spiracles and are easily seen in large caterpillars. They lead into a network of minute tubes, called tracheae, that carry air to all parts of the insect's body.

The cheetah is the world's fastest land animal and is fine-tuned for speed. It has wide nostrils to breathe in as much oxygen as possible and has specially adapted paws for running fast.

Nature's Success Story

People like to think that humans dominate Earth, but insects could, in many ways, be seen as far more successful. There are over one million species (kinds) of insects, and because they breed very quickly they can adapt to all kinds of conditions and can live just about anywhere.

Scientists divide insects into groups called orders. The insects in each order share certain features. Beetles and bugs are two of the largest insect orders. The main difference between them is that beetles have biting jaws and bugs have sucking mouthparts. So far, 350,000 different kinds of beetles and 80,000 different kinds of bugs have been found, but there are probably many more species.

Long antennae give longhorn beetles their name.

All beetles have biting jaws, located on the underside of the head.

Eyes on the front of the head give very accurate vision.

Jointed legs

Spotted longhorn beetle (*Strangalia maculata*)

Hard wing cases protect delicate rear wings.

▲ THE BEETLE ORDER

Beetles belong to the order Coleoptera, which means "sheath wings." Most beetles have two pairs of wings. The tough front wings fold over the delicate rear wings to form a hard, protective case, like body armor. Longhorn beetles owe their name to their long antennae (feelers), which look like long horns.

◄ LIVING IN WATER

Not all beetles and bugs live on land. Some, like this great diving beetle, live in freshwater ponds. The diving beetle hunts underwater, diving down to catch a variety of small creatures.

◀ FEEDING TOGETHER

A group of aphids feeds on a plant stem, sucking up liquid sap. Most beetles and bugs live alone, but a few species, such as aphids, gather together in large numbers. Some insects, such as ants and bees, form communities. Living in a group gives them protection from predators.

What's in a Name?

This image comes from the animated feature film A Bug's Life. *The hero of the cartoon is not actually a bug at all, but an ant. True bugs are a particular group of insects with sucking mouthparts that can slurp up liquid food.*

Forest shield bug
(*Pentatoma rufipes*)

Six legs keep the bug stable as it scurries along the ground.

Antennae for touching and smelling

Thin wing-tip

Hard wing base

◀ THE BUG ORDER

Bugs come in many shapes and sizes. All have long, jointed mouthparts that form a tube through which they suck up liquid food, like a syringe. Their order name is Hemiptera, which means "half-wings." The name refers to the front wings of many bugs, such as shield bugs, which are hard at the base and flimsy at the tip. With their wings folded, shield bugs are shaped like a warrior's shield.

Tube-like mouthparts under the insect's head

Eyes on the sides of the head

THE YOUNG ONES ▶

Many young insects, called larvae, look very different from the adults. This beetle larva, or grub, feeds on plant roots in the soil. Soon it will change into a winged adult. Young bugs, called nymphs, look like miniature adults when they hatch from their eggs although they have no wings.

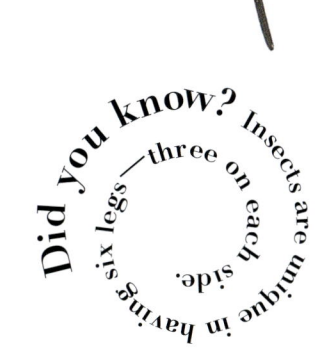

Did you know? Insects are unique in having six legs—three on each side.

Bodies in Sections

Garden chafer
(*Phyllopertha horticola*)

Head

Thorax

Abdomen

Human bodies are supported on the inside by a bony skeleton. Insects do not have bones to support them, but have a tough outer layer called an exoskeleton. This layer protects the insect's body from damage. The exoskeleton is also waterproof and helps to prevent the insect from drying out in hot weather. Holes in the exoskeleton, called spiracles, let the insect breathe.

The word "insect" comes from the Latin word *insectum* meaning "in sections." All insect bodies are made up of three main parts. They have a head, a thorax (middle section), and an abdomen (rear section). Most adult insects have one or two pairs of wings. Many of them use long antennae to sense their surroundings.

▲ **THREE SECTIONS**
This beetle's main sense organs, the antennae and eyes, are on its head. Its wings and legs are attached to the thorax. The abdomen contains the most of the digestive and reproductive organs.

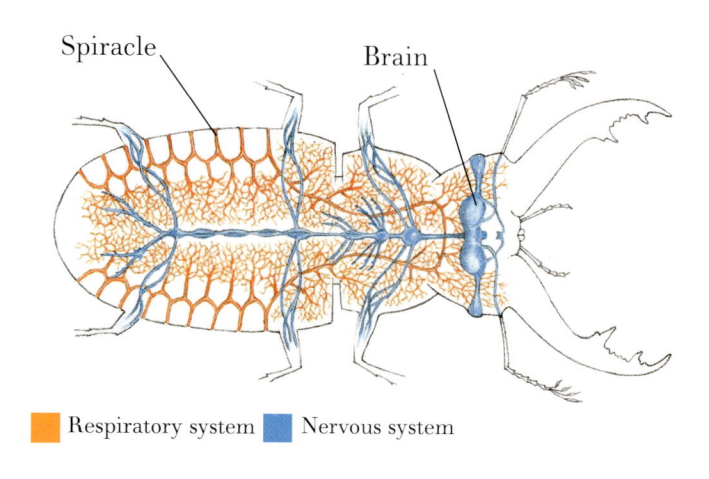

Spiracle

Brain

■ Respiratory system   ■ Nervous system

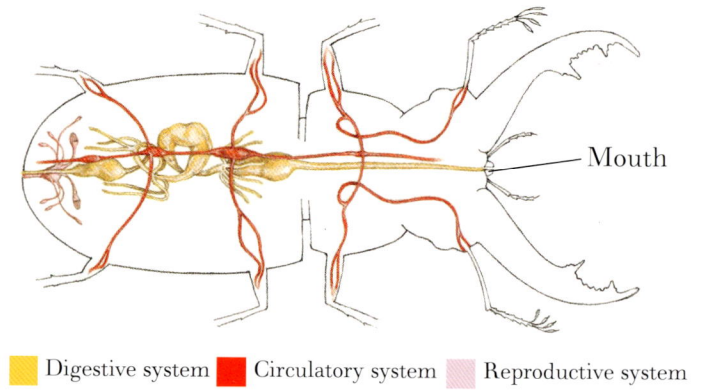

Mouth

■ Digestive system   ■ Circulatory system   ■ Reproductive system

▲ **BREATHING AND NERVOUS SYSTEMS**
The respiratory (breathing) system has spiracles (holes) that lead to a network of tubes. The tubes allow air to reach all parts of the insect's body. The nervous system receives messages from the sense organs, and sends signals to the insect's muscles to make it move.

▲ **OTHER BODY SYSTEMS**
The digestive system breaks down food and absorbs it. The circulatory system includes a long, thin heart that pumps blood through the body. The abdomen contains the reproductive parts. Males have two testes that produce sperm. Females have two ovaries that produce eggs.

◄ IN COLD BLOOD

All insects, including beetles and bugs, are cold-blooded animals. This means that the temperature of their body is similar to their surroundings. Insects control their body temperature by moving about. To warm up, many insects bask in the sun, as this leaf beetle is doing. If they need to cool their bodies, they move into the shade.

SURVIVING THE COLD ►

This tiger-beetle egg is buried in the soil. In some parts of the world, winters are too cold for adult insects to survive. The adult insects die, but their eggs, or young, survive buried in the soil. When spring arrives, the young insects emerge and become adults ready to breed before winter comes again.

Beetle Car

During the 1940s, the tough, rounded beetle shape inspired the German car manufacturer Volkswagen to produce one of the world's most popular family cars, the VW Beetle. The car's tough outer shell, just like that of a beetle, helped it to achieve a good safety record. The design proved so successful that the Beetle car was recently improved and relaunched.

Rhinoceros beetle
(*Megasoma elephas*)

▲ MOVING FORTRESS

The rhinoceros beetle is very well armored. Its tough exoskeleton covers and protects its whole body. The cuticle (outer skin) on the head and thorax of this male forms three long points that look like a rhinoceros's horns. These points are used in battles with other males over mates.

Winged Beauties

Butterflies and moths are the most beautiful of all insects. On sunny days, butterflies flit from flower to flower. Their slow, fluttering flight often reveals the full glory of their large, vividly colored wings. Moths tend to be less brightly colored than butterflies and generally fly at night.

Together, butterflies and moths make up one of the largest orders (groups) of insects, called Lepidoptera. This order includes more than 165,000 different species (kinds), living in all parts of the world except Antarctica. Most moths and butterflies feed on sugary flower nectar by dipping a long proboscis (tongue) into the heart of the flower. The proboscis is rolled up under the body when it is not being used.

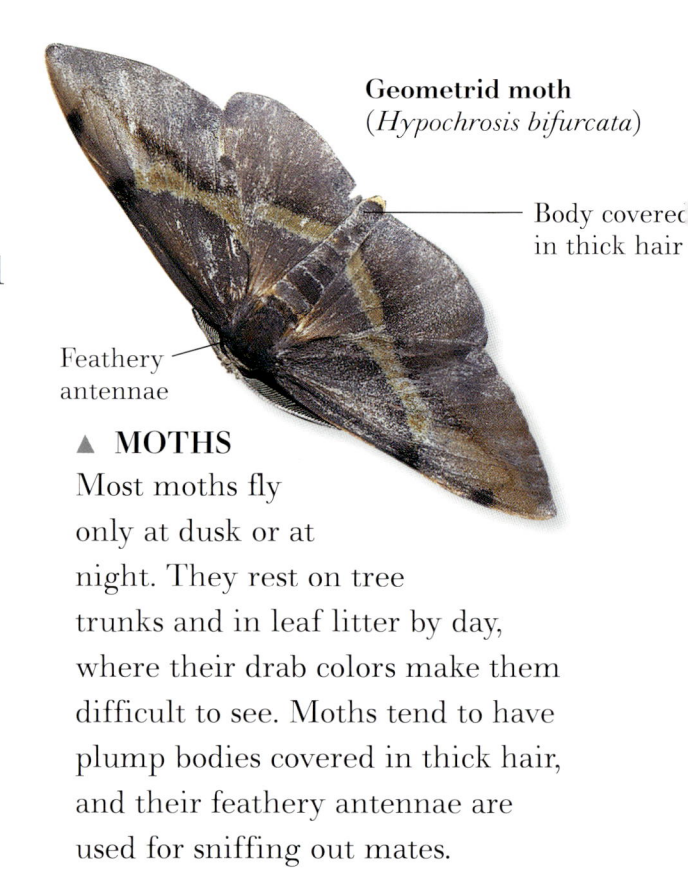

Geometrid moth
(*Hypochrosis bifurcata*)

Body covered in thick hair

Feathery antennae

▲ MOTHS
Most moths fly only at dusk or at night. They rest on tree trunks and in leaf litter by day, where their drab colors make them difficult to see. Moths tend to have plump bodies covered in thick hair, and their feathery antennae are used for sniffing out mates.

▼ RESTING BUTTERFLY
You can usually tell a butterfly from a moth by the way it folds its wings when it is resting. A moth spreads its wings back like a tent, with only the upper sides visible. However, a butterfly settles with its wings folded upright with the upper sides together, so that only the undersides show.

Green-veined white butterfly
(*Pieris napi*)

Psyche and Aphrodite
The Ancient Greeks believed that, after death, their souls fluttered away from their bodies in the form of butterflies. The Greek symbol for the soul was a butterfly-winged girl called Psyche. According to legend, Aphrodite (goddess of love) was jealous of Psyche's beauty. She ordered her son Eros to make Psyche fall in love with him. Instead, Eros fell in love with her himself.

Blue morpho butterfly
(*Morpho peleides*)

Antennae

Compound eyes
consist of up to
6,000 individual
lenses.

Brightly coloured
forewing

Wing is
covered in
overlapping
scales that
produce the
bright colors.

Tough outer coating
supports the body,
instead of an
internal skeleton.

Typical slim
body of a
butterfly

The hindwing
is smaller than
the forewing.

▲ FEATURES OF A BUTTERFLY

Butterflies tend to have brilliantly colored wings and
fly only during the day. They have slim bodies
without much hair, and their antennae are shaped
like clubs, with a lump at the end. However, the
distinction between butterflies and moths is not very
clear, and in some languages they are not
distinguished at all.

▼ CATERPILLARS

A many-legged caterpillar hatches from
a butterfly's egg. When young, both
moths and butterflies are
caterpillars. Only
when they are big
enough do the
caterpillars go
through the
changes that
turn them into
winged adults.

Privet hawk moth caterpillar
(*Sphinx ligustri*)

Did you know? Tiger moths make high-pitched clicks at night to confuse hunting bats.

Crawling Creatures

Spiders are some of the most feared and least understood creatures in the animal world. These hairy hunters are famous for spinning silk and giving a poisonous bite. There are around 35,000 known species (kinds) of spider, with probably a similar number waiting to be discovered. Only about 30 species, however, are dangerous to people. Spiders are very useful to humans, because they eat flies and other insect pests that invade our homes and yards. Spiders live nearly everywhere, from forests, deserts, and grasslands to caves. Some even live underwater. Some spin webs to catch their prey, while others leap out from a hiding place or stalk their meals like a cat. There are even spiders that fire streams of sticky silk to tangle up their prey and others that lasso flying moths.

The front part of a spider is a joined head and chest called the cephalothorax. The body is covered by a tough skin called an exoskeleton. The shield-like plate on the top of the cephalothorax is called the carapace and it carries a cluster of small eyes near the front.

Spiders use palps for holding food and as feelers.

The chelicerae (mouthparts) are used to bite and crush prey. Each ends in a fang that injects poison.

A spider's eight hollow legs are joined to the cephalothorax.

The abdomen is the rear part of a spider. It is covered by soft, stretchy skin.

Silk is spun by organs called spinnerets at the back of the abdomen.

◀ **WHAT IS A SPIDER?**
Spiders are often confused with insects, but they belong to a completely different group. A spider has eight legs, while an insect has six. Its body has two parts, while an insect's has three. Many insects have wings and antennae, but spiders do not.

WEB WEAVERS ▶

About half of all spiders spin webs. They know how to do this by instinct from birth, without being taught. Many spiders build a new web each night. They build webs to catch flying prey. Some of the web's silk is sticky to trap animals. The spider walks around on non-stick strands.

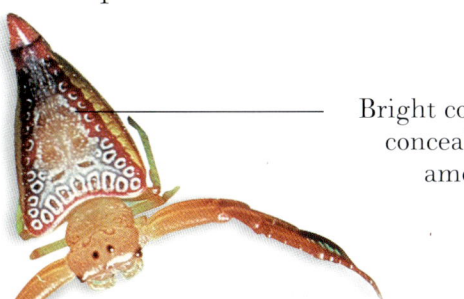

Bright colors help to conceal this spider among flowers.

▲ SPIDER SHAPES AND COLORS

The triangular spider is named after its brightly colored abdomen, which is shaped like a triangle. Its colour and shape help it to hide in wait for prey on leaves and flowers. Other spiders use bright colors to warn their enemies that they are poisonous or taste nasty.

Arachne's Tale
A Greek legend tells of Arachne, a girl who was very skilled at weaving. The goddess Athene challenged her to a contest, which Arachne won. The goddess became so cross Arachne killed herself. Athene was sorry and turned the girl into a spider so she could spin forever. The scientific name for spiders is arachnids, named after Arachne.

◀ MALES AND FEMALES

Female spiders are usually bigger than the males and not so colorful, although this female *Nephila* spider is boldly marked. The male at the top of the picture is only one-fifth of her size.

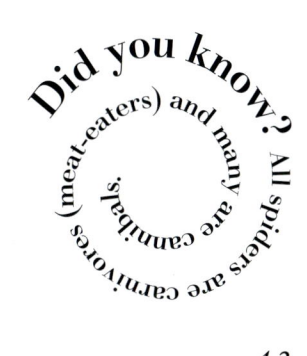

Did you know? All spiders are carnivores (meat-eaters) and many are cannibals.

How Spiders Work

From the outside, a spider's body is very different from ours. It has a tough outer skeleton, called an exoskeleton, and legs that have many joints. It has several eyes and a mouth, but no ears, nose, or tongue. Instead, it relies on a variety of hairs and bristles to touch, taste, and hear things, and it smells through microscopic pores on its feet. Inside, a spider has many features common to other animals, such as blood, nerves, a brain, and a digestive system. It also has special glands for spinning silk and for making and storing poison.

▲ **SHEDDING SKIN**
A spider's exoskeleton protects its body like a suit of armor. A waxy layer helps to make it waterproof. The exoskeleton cannot stretch as the spider grows so must be shed from time to time after a new, looser skin has grown underneath. The old skin of a huntsman spider is shown here.

Male spiders use taste hairs to pick up scent trails left by females.

◀ **HAIRY SIGNALS**
The sensitive hairs covering a spider send signals to the brain alerting it to food and enemies. Tasting hairs are spread all over the spider's body. On the palps and legs, special hairs, called trichobothria, set in cup-like sockets pick up movements in the air.

▲ **PICKING UP VIBRATIONS**
A green orb-weaver devours a fly trapped in the sticky web. Spiders use special slits on their bodies to detect when an insect is trapped in their webs. These slits, called lyriform organs, pick up vibrations caused by a struggling insect. Nerve endings in the slits send signals to the spider's brain.

SPIDER POISON ▶

A spider is a delicate creature compared to some of the prey it catches. By using poison, a spider can kill or paralyze its victim before the latter has a chance to do any harm. The spider pumps poison through its fangs. Spiders cannot chew solid food, and their poison turns the prey's body into a fleshy goo. The spider sucks up this liquid.

Poison gland linked to fang

Poison-pumping muscle

Stomach muscle

Heart

Gut

Ovary (female reproductive organ)

Rectal sac

Eyes

Chelicera (fang)

Mouth

Brain

Sucking stomach

Lung has flattened folds filled with blood, which take in oxygen.

Trachea (windpipe)

Silk glands

◀ INSIDE A SPIDER

The front part of a spider, the cephalothorax, contains the brain, poison glands, and stomach. The abdomen contains the heart, lungs, breathing tubes, gut, waste disposal system, silk glands, and reproductive organs. A spider's stomach works like a pump, stretching to pull in food that has been turned into a soupy pulp. The heart pumps blue blood around the body.

Raiko and the Earth Spider

People have regarded spiders as dangerous, magical animals for thousands of years. This Japanese print from the 1830s shows the legendary warrior Yorimitsu (also known as Raiko) and his followers slaying the fearsome Earth Spider.

Long, thin, bendy body with no legs

Tough scales protect the body and stop it drying out.

Snake Life

Snakes are reptiles, closely related to lizards and more distantly to crocodiles and turtles. Altogether, there are about 2,700 different kinds of snake, but only 300 or so are able to kill people. In Europe or North America, you are more likely to be struck by lightning than to be bitten by a poisonous snake. All snakes have long bodies covered with waterproof scales. They are meat-eaters and swallow their prey whole. Snakes have always had a special place in myths and legends, being used as symbols of both good and evil.

◄ **A SNAKE'S TAIL**
The tail of a snake is the part behind a small opening called the cloaca, where the body wastes pass out. The snake narrows slightly where the tail begins.

Tail – the part of the body that tapers off to a point

Grass snake
(*Natrix natrix*)

◄ **SNAKE HEADS**
Most snakes have a definite head and neck. But in some snakes, one end of the body looks very much like the other end!

Rattlesnake
(*Crotalus*)

◀ **FORKED TONGUE**

Snakes and some lizards have forked tongues. A snake flicks its tongue out to taste and smell the air. This gives the snake a picture of what is around it. A snake does this every few seconds if it is hunting or if there is any danger nearby.

Colombian rainbow boa
(*Epicrates cenchria maurus*)

▲ **SCALY ARMOR**

A covering of tough, dry scales grows out of a snake's skin. The scales usually hide the skin. After a big meal, the skin stretches so that it becomes visible between the scales. A snake's scales protect its body while letting it stretch, coil, and bend. The scales may be either rough or smooth.

Red-tailed boa
(*Boa constrictor*)

Did you know? Snakes never feel slimy to the touch.

Did you know? A boa squeezes its prey to death in its coils.

Medusa

An ancient Greek myth tells of Medusa, a monster with snakes for hair. Anyone who looked at her was turned to stone. Perseus managed to avoid this fate by using his polished shield to look only at the monster's reflection. He cut off Medusa's head and carried it home, dripping with blood. As each drop touched the earth, it turned into a snake.

Eye has no eyelid.

Forked tongue

**Egg-eating
snake**
(*Dasypeltis
fasciata*)

◀ **STRETCHY STOMACH**
Luckily, the throat and gut of the egg-eating
snake are so elastic that its thin body
can stretch enough
to swallow a whole
egg, shell and all.
Strong muscles in the
throat force food down
into the stomach.

Inside a Snake

A snake has a stretched-out inside to match
its long, thin outside. The backbone extends
along the whole body with hundreds of ribs joined
to it. There is not much room for organs, such as the
heart, lungs, kidneys, and liver, so they are thin shapes
to fit inside the snake's body. Many snakes have only
one lung. The stomach and gut are stretchy so that
they can hold large meals. When a snake swallows big
prey, it pushes the opening of the windpipe forward
from the back of its mouth in order to keep breathing.
Snakes are cold-blooded, which means that their
body temperature is the same as their surroundings.

Right lung is
very long and
thin and does
the work of
two lungs.

Liver is very
long and thin.

Flexible tail bone,
which extends
from the spine

▼ **SNAKE ORGANS**
This diagram shows
the inside of a male
snake. The organs are
arranged to fit the
snake's long shape. In
most backboned
animals, paired
organs, such as the
kidneys, are the
same size
and placed
opposite
each other.

▲ **RATTLER**
Rattlesnakes have dried scales on their tail. When cornered,
the snake shakes its tail to produce a warning rattle.

Rectum,
through
which waste
is passed to
the cloaca

18

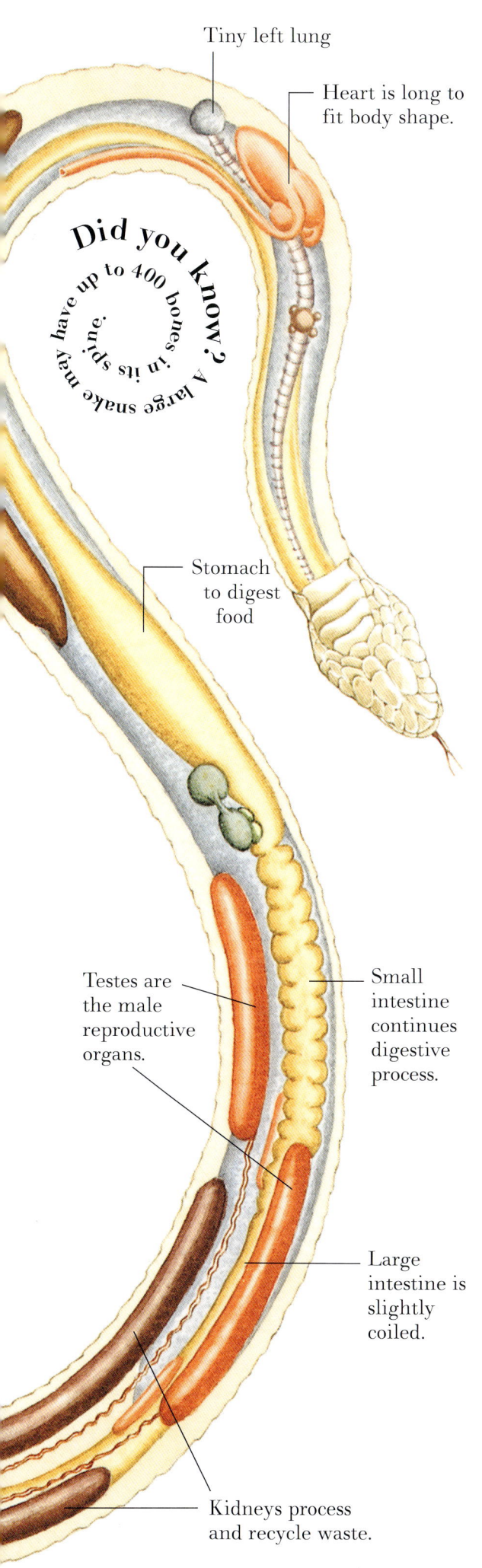

Tiny left lung

Heart is long to fit body shape.

Did you know? A large snake may have up to 400 bones in its spine.

Stomach to digest food

Testes are the male reproductive organs.

Small intestine continues digestive process.

Large intestine is slightly coiled.

Kidneys process and recycle waste.

▲ SNAKE BONES

This X-ray of a grass snake shows the delicate bones that make up its skeleton. There are no arm, leg, shoulder, or hip bones. The snake's ribs do not extend into the tail.

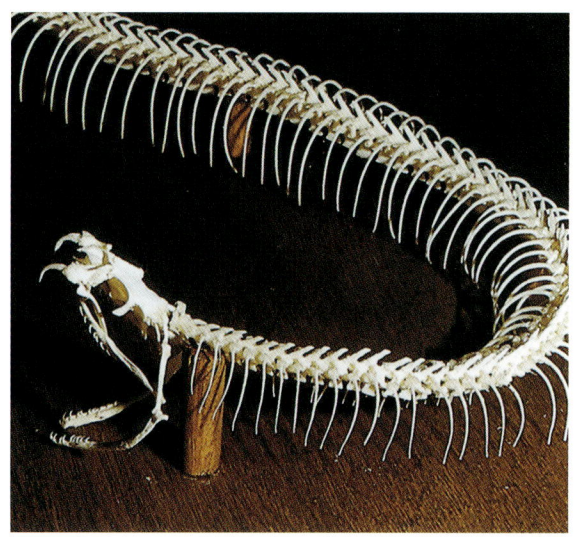

◀ SKELETON

A snake's skeleton is made up of a skull and a spine with ribs arching out from it. The jawbones can be separated so large meals can pass through.

Fierce Creatures

Crocodilians are scaly, armor-clad reptiles that include crocodiles, alligators, caimans, and gharials. They are survivors from a prehistoric age—their relatives first lived on the Earth with the dinosaurs nearly 200 million years ago. Today, they are the dinosaurs' closest living relatives, apart from birds.

Crocodilians are fierce predators. They lurk motionless in rivers, lakes, and swamps, waiting to snap up prey with their enormous jaws and sharp teeth. Their prey ranges from insects, frogs, and fish to birds and large mammals, such as deer and zebras. Crocodilians usually live in warm, tropical places in or near fresh water, but some live in the sea. They hunt and feed mainly in the water, but crawl onto dry land to sunbathe, build nests, and lay their eggs. Crocodilians rarely attack humans, even saltwater crocodiles, the largest species.

▲ SCALY TAILS

Like many crocodilians, an American alligator uses its long, strong tail to swim through the water. The tail moves from side to side to push the alligator along. The tail is the same length as the rest of the body.

Long, strong tail has flat sides to push aside water for swimming.

CROCODILIAN CHARACTERISTICS ▶

With its thick, scaly skin, huge jaws, and powerful tail, this American alligator looks like a living dinosaur. Its eyes and nostrils are on top of its head so that it can see and breathe when the rest of its body is underwater. On land, crocodilians slither along on their bellies, but they can lift themselves up on their four short legs to walk.

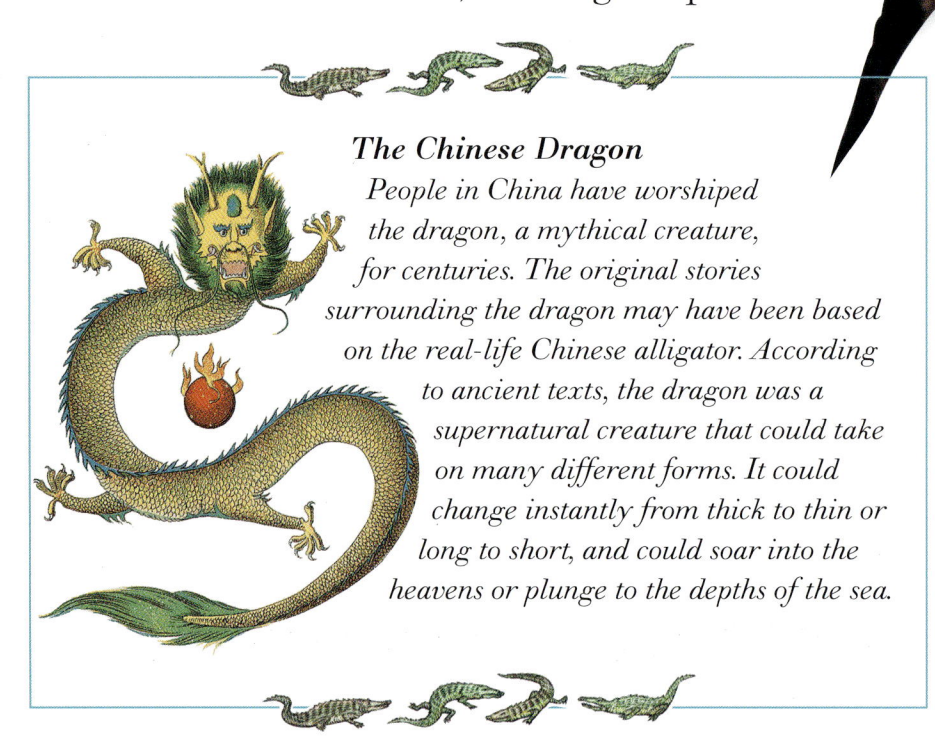

The Chinese Dragon

People in China have worshiped the dragon, a mythical creature, for centuries. The original stories surrounding the dragon may have been based on the real-life Chinese alligator. According to ancient texts, the dragon was a supernatural creature that could take on many different forms. It could change instantly from thick to thin or long to short, and could soar into the heavens or plunge to the depths of the sea.

▲ TALKING HEADS

Huge, powerful jaws lined with sharp teeth make Nile crocodiles killing machines. They are some of the world's largest and most dangerous reptiles. The teeth are used to attack and grip prey, but are useless for chewing. Prey has to be swallowed whole or in chunks.

SHUTEYE ►

Although this spectacled caiman has its eyes shut, it is probably not asleep, just resting. Two butterflies are basking in safety on the caiman's head. Animals will not dare to come near because the caiman is still sensitive to what is going on around it, even though its eyes are shut.

SOAKING UP THE SUN ►

Nile crocodiles sun themselves on a sandbank. This is called basking and it warms the body. Crocodilians are cold-blooded, which means that their body temperature is affected by their surroundings. They have no fur or feathers to keep them warm, nor can they shiver to warm up. They sunbathe to warm themselves and slip into the water to cool down.

The scales on the back are usually much more bony than those on the belly.

Scaly skin covers the whole body for protection and camouflage.

Did you know? Most crocodilians live for about 50 years but some live up to 100.

Eyes and nostrils are on top of the head.

The digits (toes) of each foot are slightly webbed.

American alligator (*Alligator mississippiensis*)

Long snout with sharp teeth to catch prey.

Crocodilian Bodies

The crocodilian body has changed very little over the last 200 million years. It is superbly adapted to life in the water. Crocodilians can breathe with just their nostrils above the surface. Underwater, ears and nostrils close and a transparent third eyelid sweeps across the eye for protection. Crocodilians are the only reptiles with ear flaps. Inside the long, lizard-like body, a bony skeleton supports and protects the lungs, heart, stomach, and other soft organs. The stomach is in two parts, one part for grinding food, the other for absorbing (taking in) nutrients. Unlike other reptiles, which have a three-chambered heart, a crocodilian's heart has four chambers, like a mammal's. This stronger heart can pump more oxygen-rich blood to the brain during a dive. The thinking part of its brain is more developed than in other reptiles, and crocodilians learn their hunting skills rather than just acting on instinct.

▲ **THROAT FLAP**
A crocodilian has no lips so it is unable to seal its mouth underwater. Instead, two special flaps at the back of the throat stop water flowing from its mouth into its lungs. This enables the crocodile to open its mouth underwater to catch and eat prey without drowning.

Did you know? A saltwater crocodile can stay underwater for more than an hour.

◄ **OPEN WIDE**
Crocodilians have mighty jaws. However, the muscles that close the mouth are much stronger than the ones that open it. This American alligator is relaxing with its mouth agape. Gaping helps to cool the animal down.

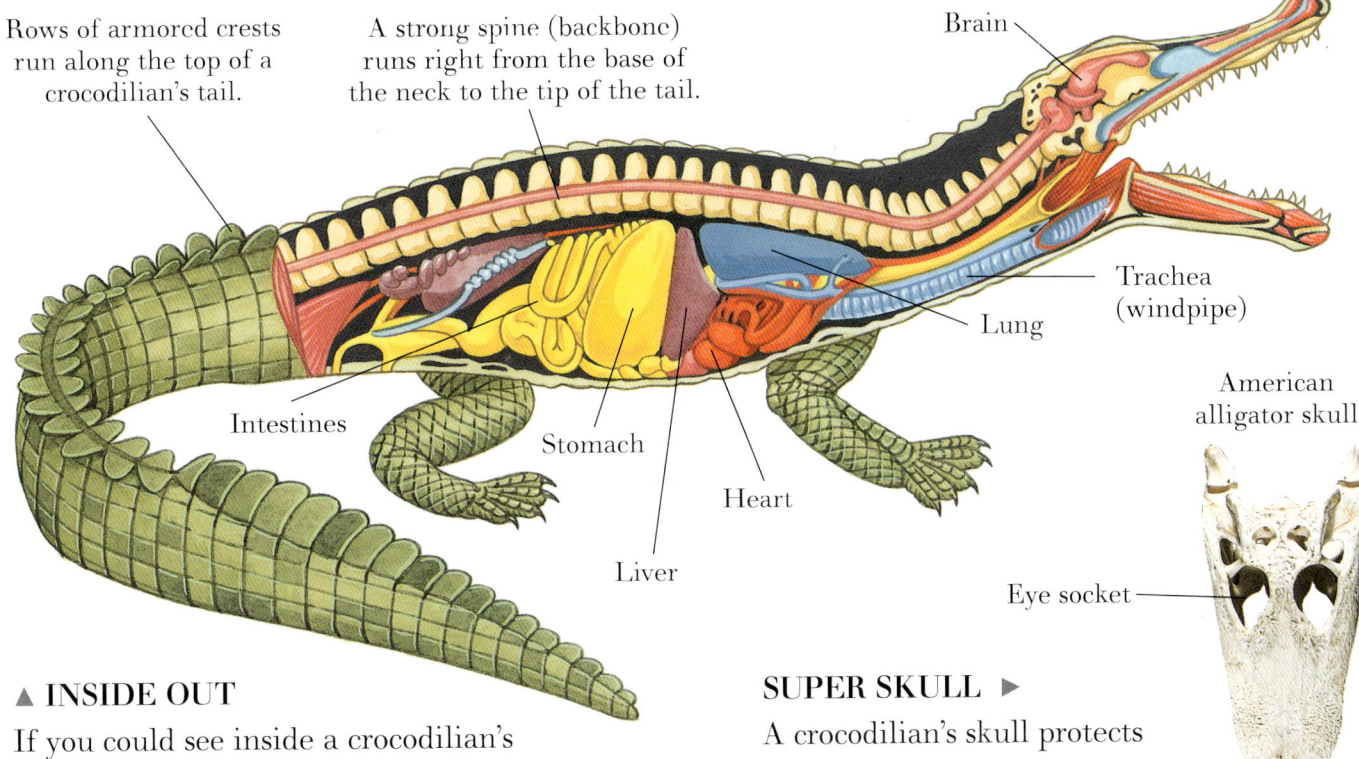

Rows of armored crests run along the top of a crocodilian's tail.

A strong spine (backbone) runs right from the base of the neck to the tip of the tail.

Brain

Trachea (windpipe)

Lung

Intestines

Stomach

Heart

Liver

American alligator skull

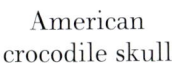

Eye socket

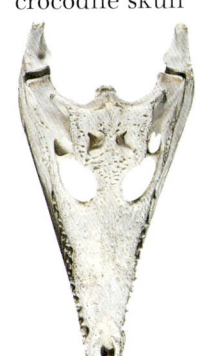

American crocodile skull

▲ INSIDE OUT

If you could see inside a crocodilian's body, you would see a mixture of reptile, bird, and mammal features. The crocodilian's brain and shoulder blades are like a bird's. Its heart, diaphragm, and efficient breathing system are similar to those of mammals. The stomach and digestive system are those of a reptile, as they deal with food in unchewed chunks.

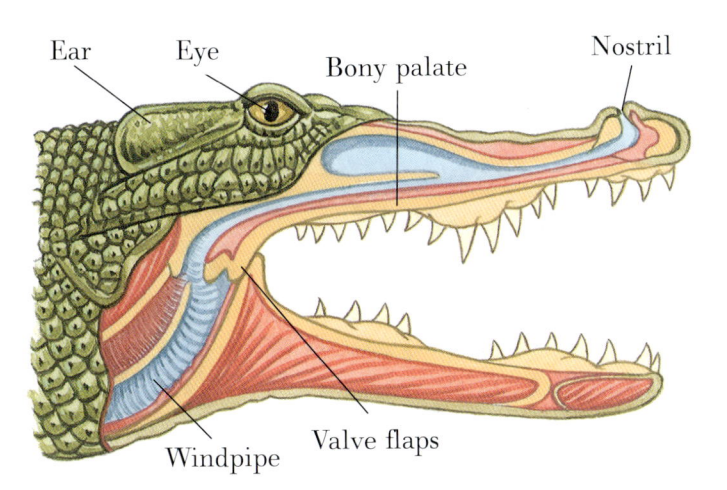

Ear

Eye

Bony palate

Nostril

Windpipe

Valve flaps

▲ WELL DESIGNED

A view inside the head of a crocodilian shows the ear, eye, and nostril openings set high up in the skull. The bones in the roof of the mouth are joined together to create a bony palate that separates the nostrils from the mouth. Flaps of skin form a valve, sealing off the windpipe underwater.

SUPER SKULL ▶

A crocodilian's skull protects the animal's large reptile brain. The skull is wider and more rounded in alligators (*top*), and long and triangular in crocodiles (*bottom*). Behind the eye sockets are two large holes where strong jaw muscles emerge and attach to the outer surface of the skull.

▶ STOMACH STONES

Crocodilians swallow objects, such as pebbles, to help mash up their food. These gastroliths (stomach stones) churn around inside part of the stomach, helping to break up food so it can be digested. Not all gastroliths are stones. Bottles, coins, and a whistle have been found inside crocodilians.

23

Winged Hunters

There are nearly 9,000 different species (kinds) of birds in the world. Most of them eat plant shoots, seeds, nuts, and fruit, or small creatures such as insects and worms. However, around 400 species, called birds of prey, hunt larger creatures or scavenge carrion (the flesh of dead animals). Birds of prey are called raptors, from the Latin *rapere* meaning "to seize," because they grip and kill their prey with sharp talons (claws) and hooked beaks. Raptors have very sharp eyes and good hearing, so they can locate their prey on the wing. Most raptors, including eagles, falcons, and hawks hunt by day. Vultures are active in the day, too, searching for carrion. Owls are raptors that hunt by night.

▼ HANGING AROUND

The outstretched wings of the kestrel face into the wind as the bird hovers like a kite above a patch of ground in search of a meal. The bird also spreads the feathers of its broad tail to keep it steady in the wind.

Large, forward-facing eyes

Hooked, powerful bill

▼ IN A LEAGUE OF THEIR OWN

Five young tawny owls cluster together on a branch. Owls are not closely related to the other birds of prey. However, like other raptors, they have talons, hooked beaks, and excellent eyesight. Most hunt silently during the hours of darkness. Their rounded faces act like satellite dishes that collect the slightest sounds and direct them to the birds' ears.

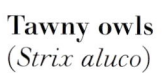

Tawny owls
(*Strix aluco*)

◀ HAWKEYE

The sparrowhawk has large eyes that face forward. The bill is hooked, for tearing flesh. These are typical features of daytime hunters.

Eurasian sparrowhawk
(*Accipiter nisus*)

Long, sharp, curved talons

Wings lift in the flow of air and support the bird's weight. The primary feathers on the wing fan out.

Tail guides the bird through the air and also acts as a brake.

▲ BUILT FOR SPEED

The peregrine falcon is one of the swiftest birds in the world, able to dive at up to 140 miles per hour. Its swept-back wings help it cut through the air at speed. Their shape has been copied by designers for the wings of fighter planes.

▼ THE EAGLE HAS LANDED

In the snow-covered highlands of Scotland, a golden eagle stands over a rabbit it has just killed. Eagles kill with their talons, which are so long, sharp, and deeply curved that one swipe is usually enough to kill the rabbit.

Golden eagle
(*Aquila chrysaetos*)

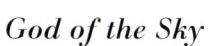

God of the Sky

Horus was one of the most important gods in ancient Egypt. He was the god of the sky and the heavens. His sacred bird was the falcon, and Horus is often represented with a human body and a falcon's head. The Egyptian hieroglyph (picture symbol) for "god" in ancient Egyptian is a falcon.

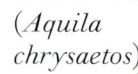

How Birds of Prey Work

Birds of prey are expert fliers. Like other birds, they have powerful chest and wing muscles to move their wings. Virtually the whole body is covered with feathers to make it smooth so that it can slip easily through the air. The bones are very light, and some have a honeycomb structure, which makes them even lighter but still very strong. Birds of prey differ from other birds in a number of ways, particularly in their powerful bills (beaks) and clawed feet, which are well adapted for their life as hunters. Also, like many other birds, they regurgitate (cough up) pellets. These contain the parts of their prey they cannot digest.

▲ NAKED NECK

A Ruppell's vulture feeds on a zebra carcass in the Masai Mara region of eastern Africa. Like many vultures, it has a naked neck, which it can thrust deep inside the carcass. As a result, it can feed without getting its feathers too covered in blood.

◄ BODY PARTS

Underneath their feathery covering, birds of prey have a complex system of internal organs. Unlike humans, most birds have a crop to store food in before digestion. They also have a gizzard to grind up hard particles of food, such as bone, and to start the process of making a pellet. Birds also have a syrinx (the bird equivalent of the human voice box).

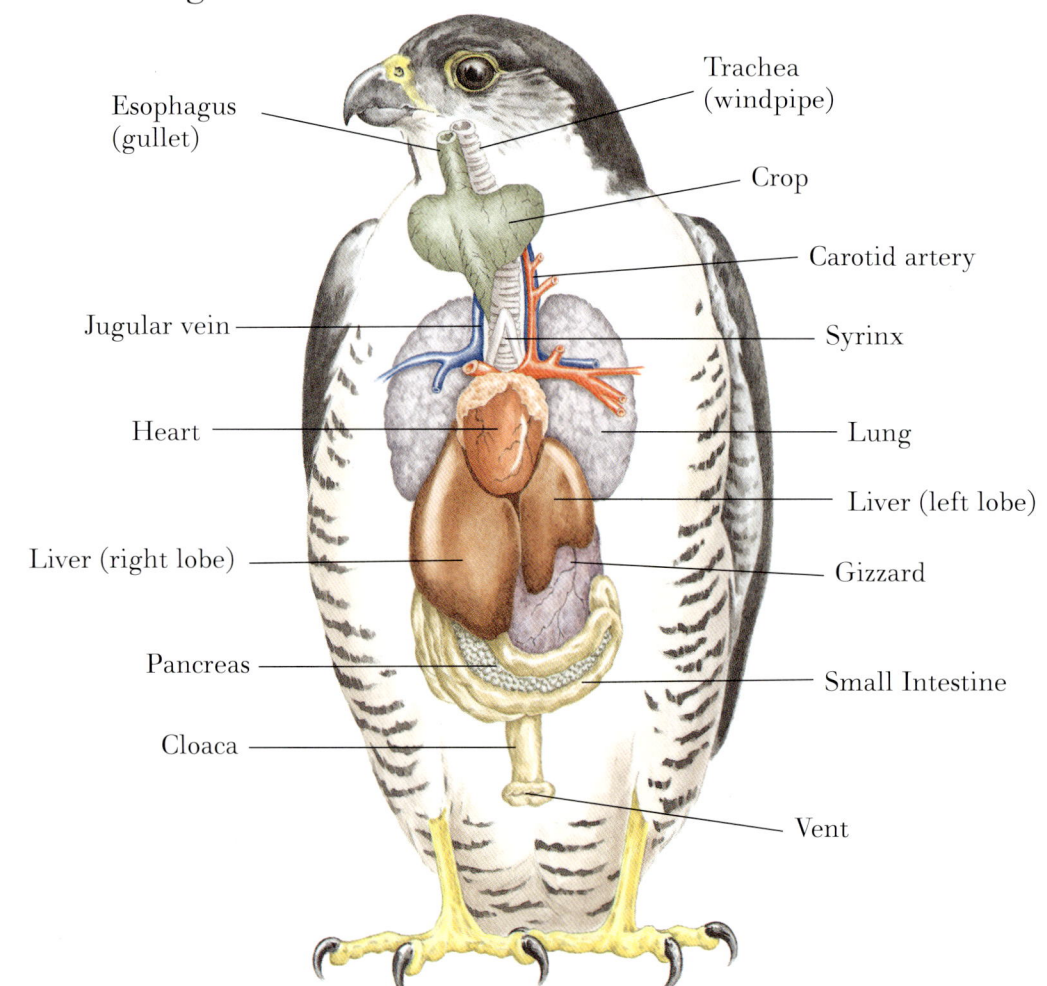

Esophagus (gullet)

Trachea (windpipe)

Crop

Carotid artery

Jugular vein

Syrinx

Heart

Lung

Liver (left lobe)

Liver (right lobe)

Gizzard

Pancreas

Small Intestine

Cloaca

Vent

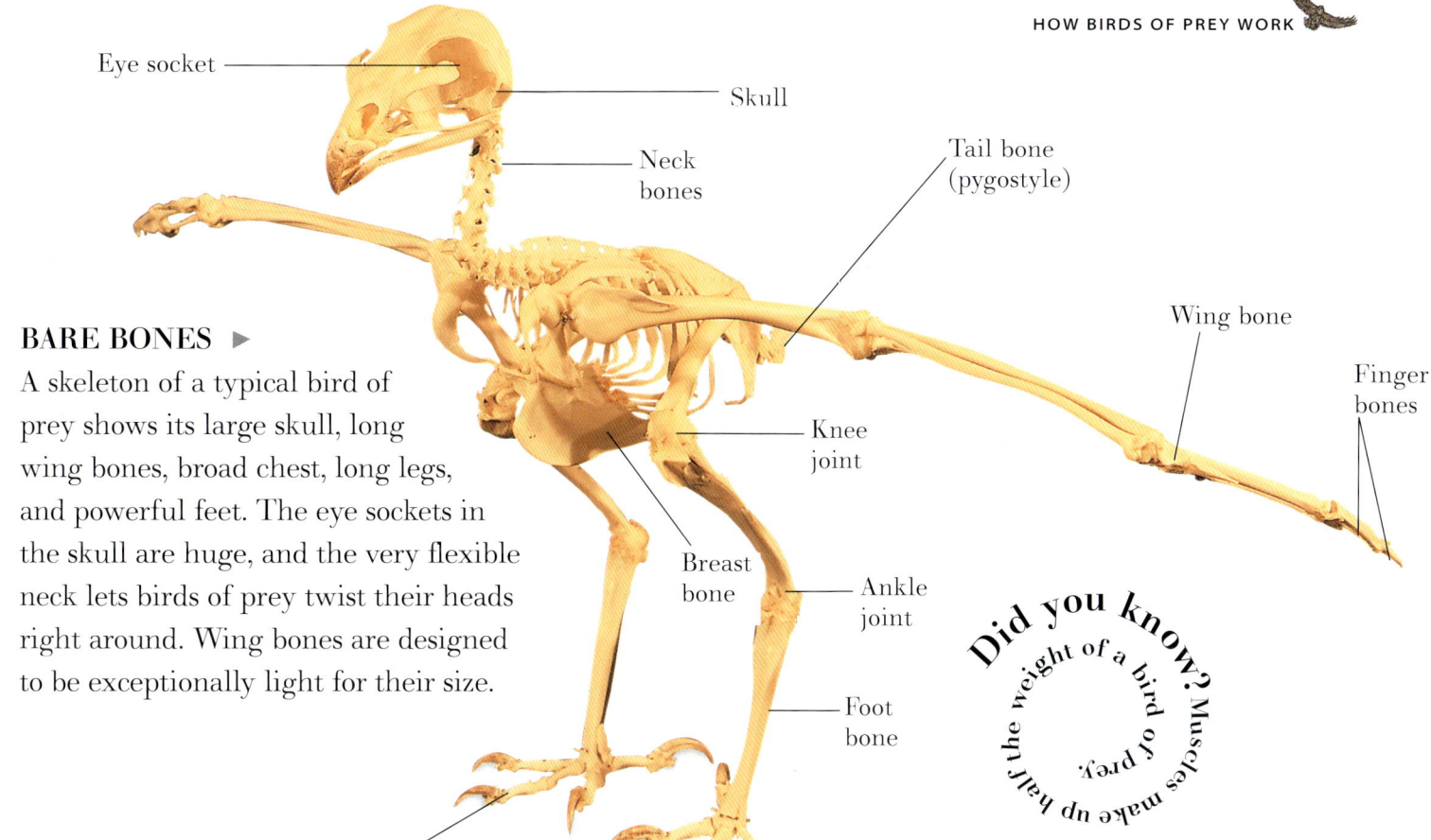

Eye socket

Skull

Neck bones

Tail bone (pygostyle)

Wing bone

Finger bones

Knee joint

Breast bone

Ankle joint

Foot bone

Toe

Talon

BARE BONES ▶

A skeleton of a typical bird of prey shows its large skull, long wing bones, broad chest, long legs, and powerful feet. The eye sockets in the skull are huge, and the very flexible neck lets birds of prey twist their heads right around. Wing bones are designed to be exceptionally light for their size.

Did you know? Muscles make up half the weight of a bird of prey.

▼ BACK TO FRONT

This peregrine falcon appears to have eyes in the back of its head. Its body is facing away, but its eyes are looking straight into the camera. All birds of prey can twist their heads right around like this, because they have many more neck bones than mammals. They can see in any direction without moving their body, but they cannot move their eyeballs in their sockets.

Peregrine falcon (*Falco peregrinus*)

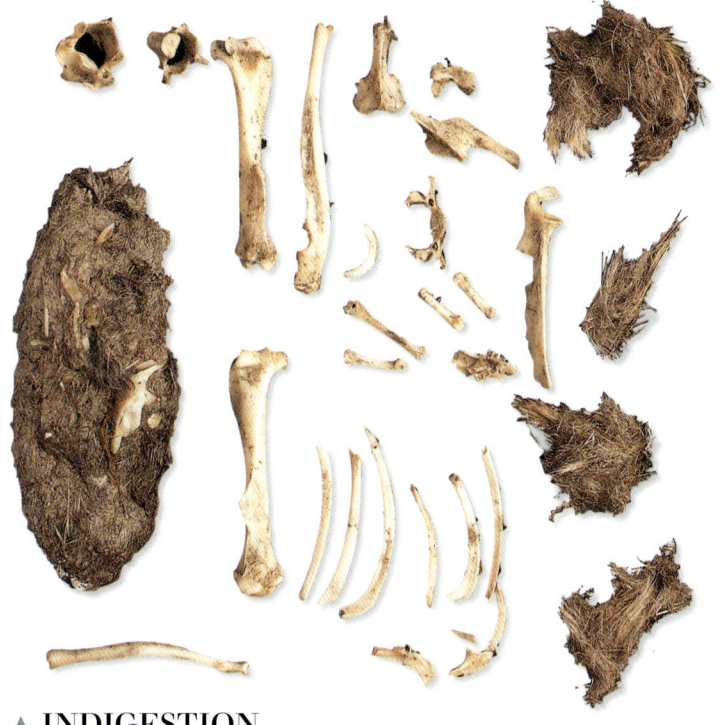

▲ INDIGESTION

On the left of the picture above is the regurgitated (coughed-up) pellet of a barn owl, and on the right are the indigestible parts it contained. The pellet is about 2 inches long. From the scraps of fur and fragments of bone in it, we can tell that the owl has just eaten a small mammal.

27

Built for Speed

Equids are designed to be able to flee from predators. Their skeletons are lightweight, strong, and geared for maximum speed with minimum energy. A horse's upper leg bones, for example, are fused into a single, strong bone, while in humans their equivalents are two separate bones. The joints are less flexible than those of a human. Instead, they are strong in an up-and-down direction to support and protect powerful tendons and muscles. A horse's skeleton is designed to absorb the weight and impact of its body as it moves over the ground.

▲ RESTING ON AUTOMATIC

When horses are standing at rest, the patella (kneecap) slots into a groove in the femur (leg bone). This locks their back legs into an energy-saving position, just like our knees. Another mechanism keeps the horse's head from dropping to the ground. A ligament in the neck acts like a piece of elastic, returning the head to an upright resting position when the horse is not grazing.

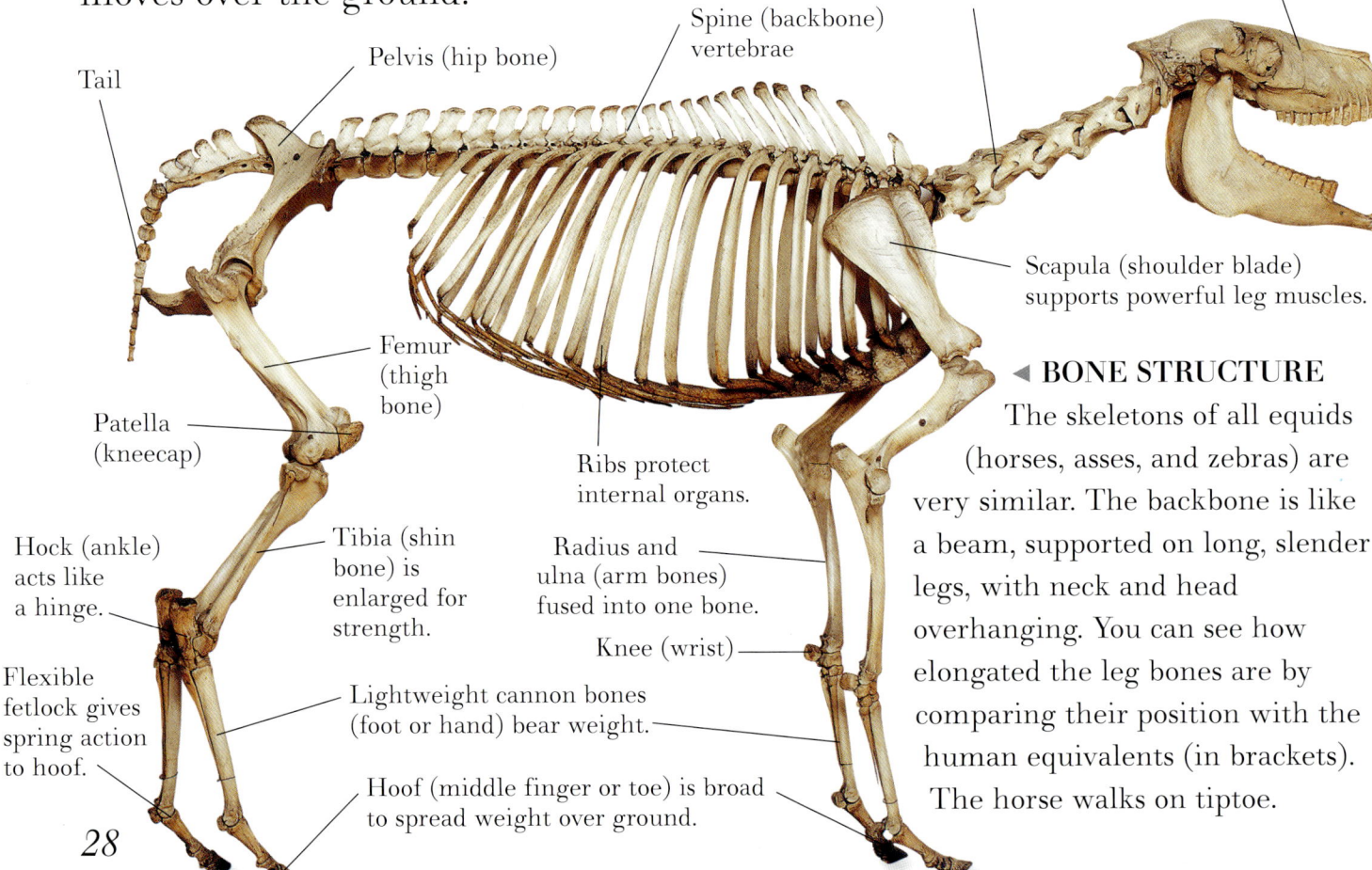

Long neck vertebrae make grazing easy.

Long, narrow skull

Spine (backbone) vertebrae

Tail

Pelvis (hip bone)

Scapula (shoulder blade) supports powerful leg muscles.

Femur (thigh bone)

Patella (kneecap)

◄ BONE STRUCTURE

The skeletons of all equids (horses, asses, and zebras) are very similar. The backbone is like a beam, supported on long, slender legs, with neck and head overhanging. You can see how elongated the leg bones are by comparing their position with the human equivalents (in brackets). The horse walks on tiptoe.

Ribs protect internal organs.

Hock (ankle) acts like a hinge.

Tibia (shin bone) is enlarged for strength.

Radius and ulna (arm bones) fused into one bone.

Knee (wrist)

Flexible fetlock gives spring action to hoof.

Lightweight cannon bones (foot or hand) bear weight.

Hoof (middle finger or toe) is broad to spread weight over ground.

28

◀ SPACE FOR CHEWING

The long and narrow skull provides space for the big molar teeth, and enables the eye sockets to fit in behind them. This means that when the horse chews, there is no pressure on the eye. The large eye sockets give enough space for the horse to have all-round vision.

▼ FIGHTING TEETH

The small tushes (or tusker) teeth, just behind the big incisors, are used in fights between stallions (males). Mares (females) have very small tushes teeth or none at all.

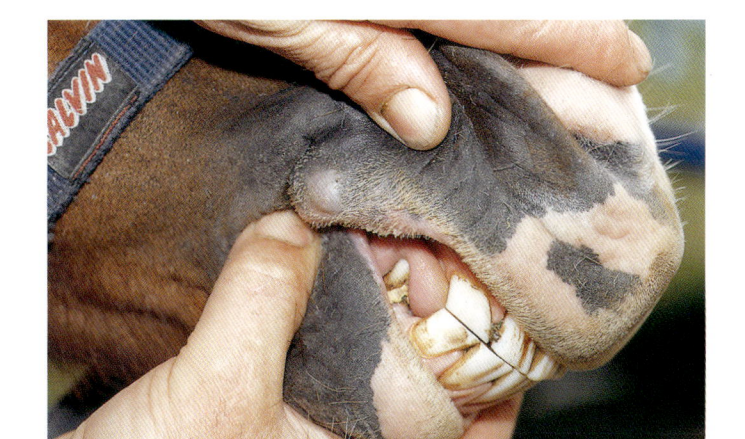

Pegasus

Greek mythology tells of a winged horse called Pegasus. He sprang fully grown from the dead body of the evil Medusa after she was beheaded. Pegasus was ridden by the hero Bellerophon. Together they defeated the fire-breathing monster, the Chimera. Bellerophon tried to ride Pegasus to heaven, but the gods were angry and he was thrown off and killed. Pegasus became a constellation in the night sky.

TEETH FOR THE JOB ▶

Mares have 36–40 teeth and stallions 44 teeth. A horse's teeth are specially adapted for its diet. Chisel-shaped incisors at the front snip through grass. Molars in the side of the mouth grind down the grass before it is swallowed. The degree of wear on teeth is sometimes used to calculate a horse's age. This can be misleading, as some foods wear down the teeth more than others do.

Powerful Bodies

The horse is one of the fastest long-distance runners in the animal world. Its digestive system processes large quantities of food in order to extract sufficient energy. The digestive system is in two parts. The food is partly digested in the stomach, then moves quickly through to the hindgut (cecum and colon). Here, bacteria break down the tough cell walls of the plants. The nutrients are released, and cells lining the gut are ready to absorb them.

Equids also have a big heart and large lungs. This lets them run quickly and over a long distance. Horse tendons connecting muscles to bones are very elastic, especially those in the lower leg. Together with the ligaments, which bind bones together at joints, they can stretch and give to save energy and cushion impact of the hooves on the ground when the horse is on the move.

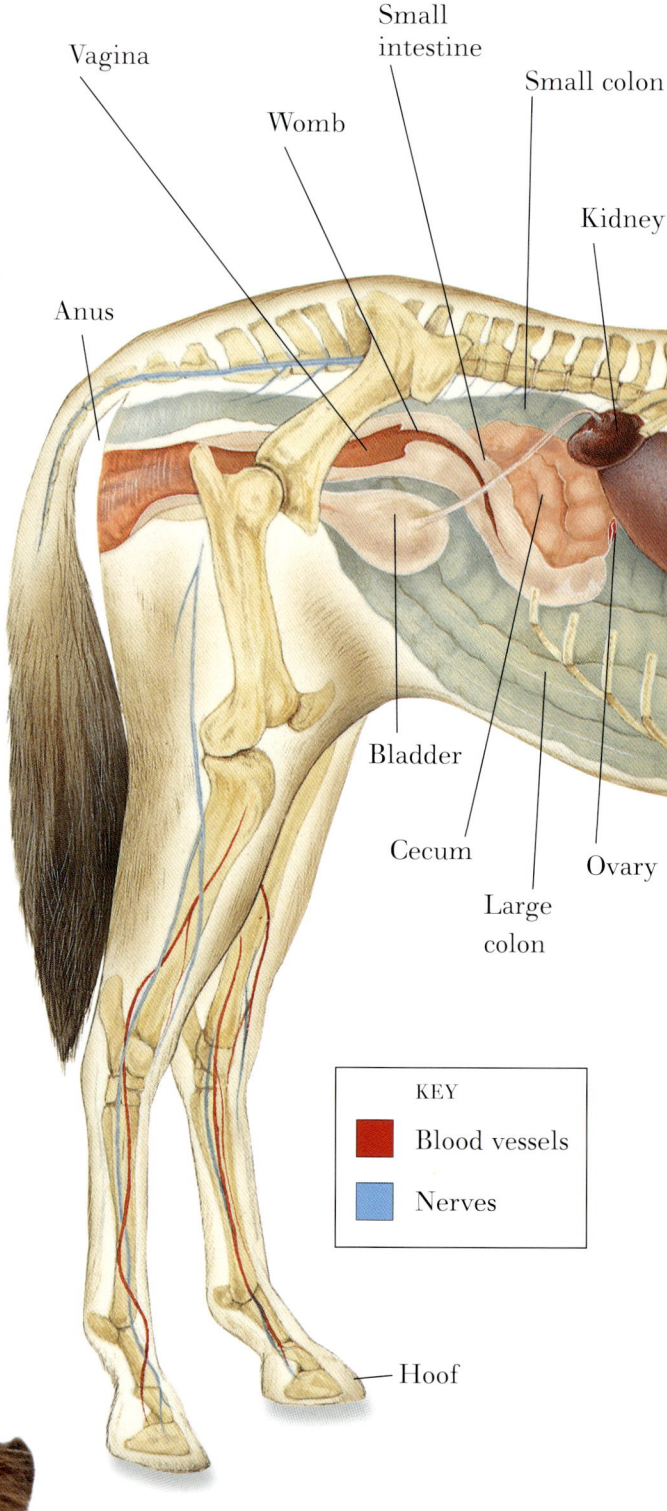

Vagina
Small intestine
Small colon
Womb
Kidney
Anus
Bladder
Cecum
Ovary
Large colon
Hoof

KEY
Blood vessels
Nerves

◄ FLEXIBLE LIPS

The horse's mobile, sensitive lips are described as prehensile (able to grasp). They are used to select and pick food. When a horse wants to use its power of smell to full effect, it curls its lips back.

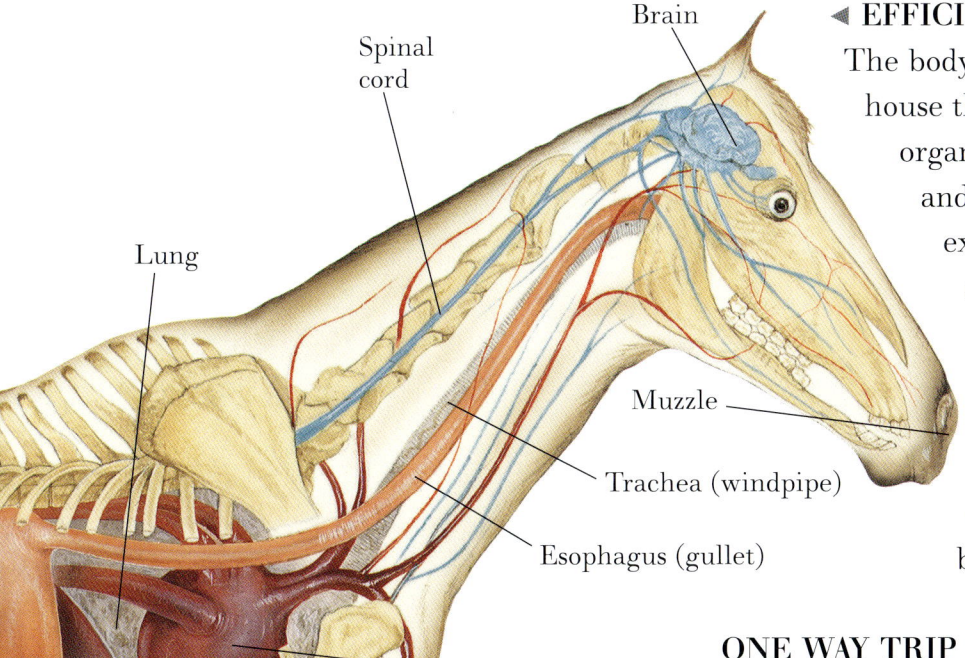

Spinal
cord

Brain

Lung

Muzzle

Trachea (windpipe)

Esophagus (gullet)

Heart

Liver

Stomach

Spleen

◄ EFFICIENT BODYWORKS

The body of the horse is big enough to house the powerful muscles and large organs that the animal needs for speed and endurance. The large heart, for example, pumps at 30–40 beats per minute when resting—about half the rate of a human's. This can rise to a top rate of 240—nearly twice the rate of a human's—when working hard. This means that blood circulates around the body very efficiently.

ONE WAY TRIP ►

Horses eat almost continuously, and have an extra-long digestive tract—around 98 feet—to get as much benefit as possible from their low-grade diet. They cannot vomit because one-way valves in the stomach prevent food from being regurgitated. Eating something poisonous could, therefore, be fatal.

LONG LEGS ►

Horses' feet have a single toe, tipped with a fingernail-like hoof. Horses stand on this single toe. Their heel bone never touches the ground, making their legs very long— ideal for running and jumping.

Gentle Giants

Elephants are the largest and heaviest creatures on land. An African male (bull) elephant weighs as much as 80 people, six automobiles, 12 horses, or 1,500 cats. Elephants are extremely strong and can pick up whole trees with their trunks. They are also highly intelligent, gentle animals. Females live together in family groups and look after one another. Elephants are mammals—they can control their body temperature and they feed milk to their babies. After humans, elephants are the longest lived of all mammals. Some live to be about 70 years old. Two species (kinds) of elephant exist today—the African elephant and the Asian elephant. Both have a trunk, thick skin, and large ears, although African elephants have larger ears than Indian ones. Not all elephants have tusks, however. Generally, only African elephants and male Asian elephants have tusks.

▲ **WORKING ELEPHANTS**
In India, domesticated (tamed) elephants are used by farmers to carry heavy loads. In some Asian countries they also move heavy logs by pulling them.

Indra and the Elephant
One of the most celebrated Hindu gods, Indra, rides a mighty white elephant called Airavata. In Hinduism (the main religion of India), elephants are sacred animals. One of Indra's emblems is the ankus, a special pointed stick used to control elephants. Indra is shown holding an ankus in this painting.

Tail, has a brush of thick hair at the end.

African elephant (*Loxodonta africana*)

▼ UNUSUAL FEATURES

The mighty elephant is a record-breaking beast. Not only is it the largest land animal, it is also the second tallest—only the giraffe is taller. It has larger ears, teeth, and tusks than any other animal. The elephant is also one of the few animals to have a nose in the form of a long trunk.

FAMILY LIFE ▲

Adult male and female elephants do not live together in family groups. Instead, adult sisters and daughters live in groups led by an older female. Adult males (bulls) live on their own or in all-male groups.

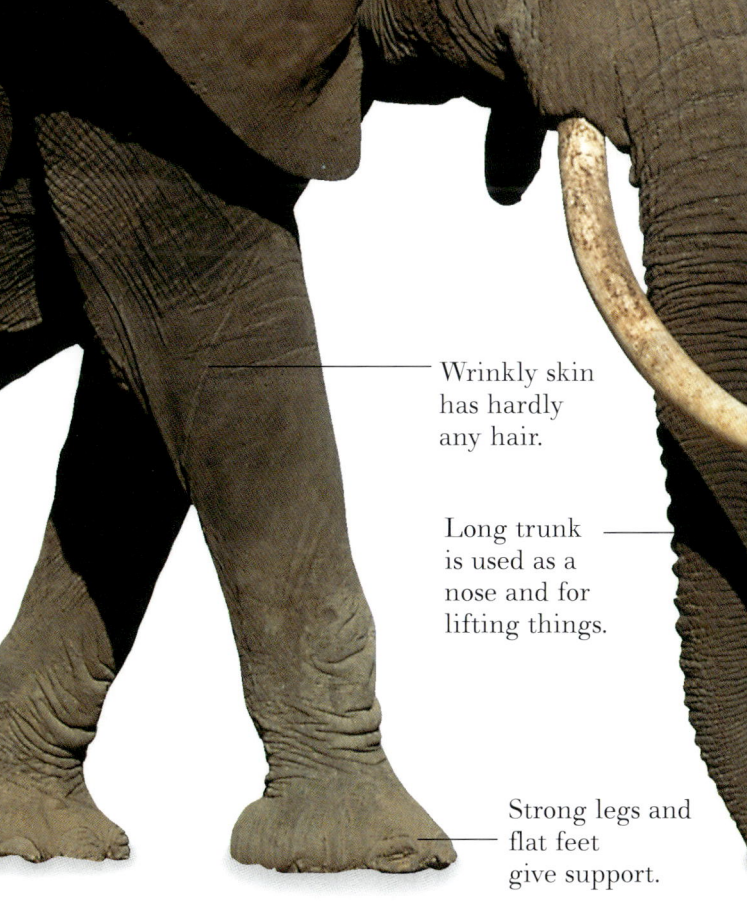

Huge ear is flapped to keep the elephant cool.

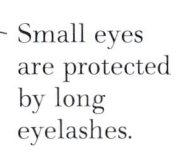
Small eyes are protected by long eyelashes.

Wrinkly skin has hardly any hair.

Long trunk is used as a nose and for lifting things.

Gently curved tusks are used for digging, fighting, and lifting.

Strong legs and flat feet give support.

BABY ELEPHANTS ▲

An elephant baby feels safe between its mother's front legs. It spends most of the first year of its life there. Mother elephants look after their young for longer than any other animal parent except humans. Daughters never leave the family group unless the group becomes too big.

Elephant Bodies

An elephant's skin is thick, gray, and wrinkly, and surprisingly sensitive. Some insects, including flies and mosquitoes, can bite through it. Often, elephants roll around in the mud to keep flies from biting them (as well as cooling themselves down). Underneath the skin, the elephant has typical mammal body parts, only very large. The heart is about five times bigger than a human heart and weighs up to 46 pounds—the weight of a small child. Also, an elephant's huge intestines can weigh nearly a ton, including the contents. The powerful lungs are operated by strong muscles. These let the elephant breathe underwater while using its trunk as a snorkel.

▲ PINK SKIN
An elephant gets its color from dots of gray pigment (coloring) in the skin. As it ages, this gray pigment may gradually fade so that the skin looks pink.

▲ THICK SKIN
An elephant's skin is 1 inch thick on the back and in some areas of the head. But in other places, such as around the mouth, the skin is paper thin.

Did you know? Some very rare Asian elephants have white skin.

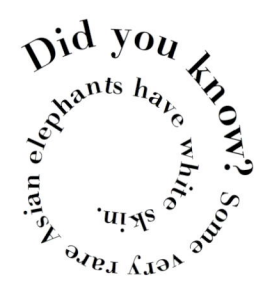

◄ ELEPHANT HAIR
The hairiest part of an elephant is the end of its tail. The tail hairs are many times thicker than human hair and grow into thick tufts. Apart from the end of the tail, the chin, and around the eyes and ears, the adult elephant has very little hair.

▲ FLY SWATTER

Although they can swish their tufted tails to get rid of flies, elephants also use leafy branches to swat annoying insect pests. They pick a branch up with their trunks and brush it across their backs to wipe the pests away.

Flying Elephants
According to an Indian folk tale, elephants could once fly. This ability was taken away by a hermit with magical powers when a flock of elephants woke him from a deep trance. The elephants landed in a tree above him, making a lot of noise and causing a branch to fall on his head. The hermit was so furious that he cast a magical spell.

▼ INSIDE AN ELEPHANT

If you could look inside the body of an elephant, you would see its huge skeleton supporting the organs. The cross-section shown here is of a female African elephant.

Ribs

Small intestine

Ovaries

Shoulder blade

Brain

Skull

Eye

Nostril

Backbone (spine)

Kidney

Uterus

Bladder

Esophagus (gullet)

Trachea (windpipe)

Lung

Stomach

Liver

Large intestine

Anus

Nerve in trunk

Heart

Wrist bone

Nerve

Blood vessel

Ankle bone

35

Big Bones

An elephant's legs are placed directly underneath its body, like a table's legs. This arrangement provides a firm support for its great weight. The leg bones stack one above the other to form a strong pillar. As a result, an elephant can rest, and even sleep, while standing up. The pillar-like legs also help to hold up the backbone, which runs along the top of the animal and supports the ribs. The backs of Asian elephants arch upward, while African elephants' backs have a dip in them. These different shapes are produced by bones that stick up from the backbone. The elephant's skeleton is not just built for strength, however. It is also flexible enough to let the elephant kneel and squat.

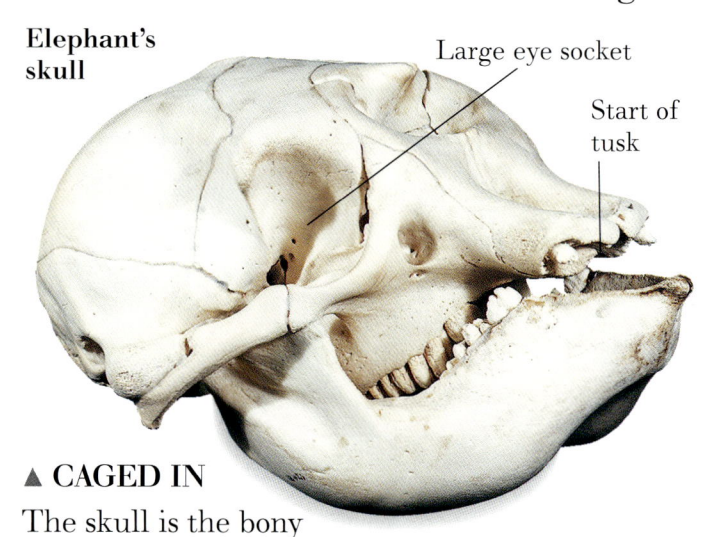

▲ BONY BACK

Crests of bone stick up from the backbone of the Asian elephant's skeleton. The muscles that hold up the head are joined to these spines and to the back of the skull.

Elephant's skull

Large eye socket

Start of tusk

▲ CAGED IN

The skull is the bony box that protects the brain and holds the huge teeth and tusks. The skull above is that of a young male elephant with undeveloped tusks. On an adult male, the upper jaw juts out farther than the lower jaw because it contains the roots for the heavy tusks.

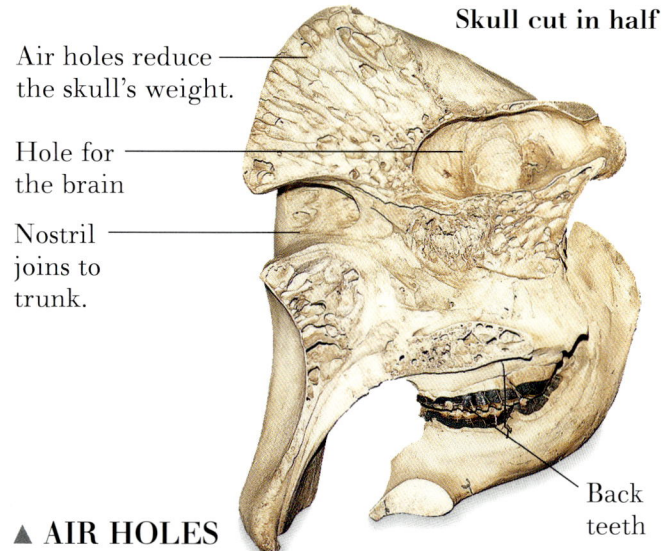

Skull cut in half

Air holes reduce the skull's weight.

Hole for the brain

Nostril joins to trunk.

Back teeth

▲ AIR HOLES

An elephant has a large skull compared to the size of its body. However, a honeycomb of air holes inside the skull makes it lighter than it looks from the outside.

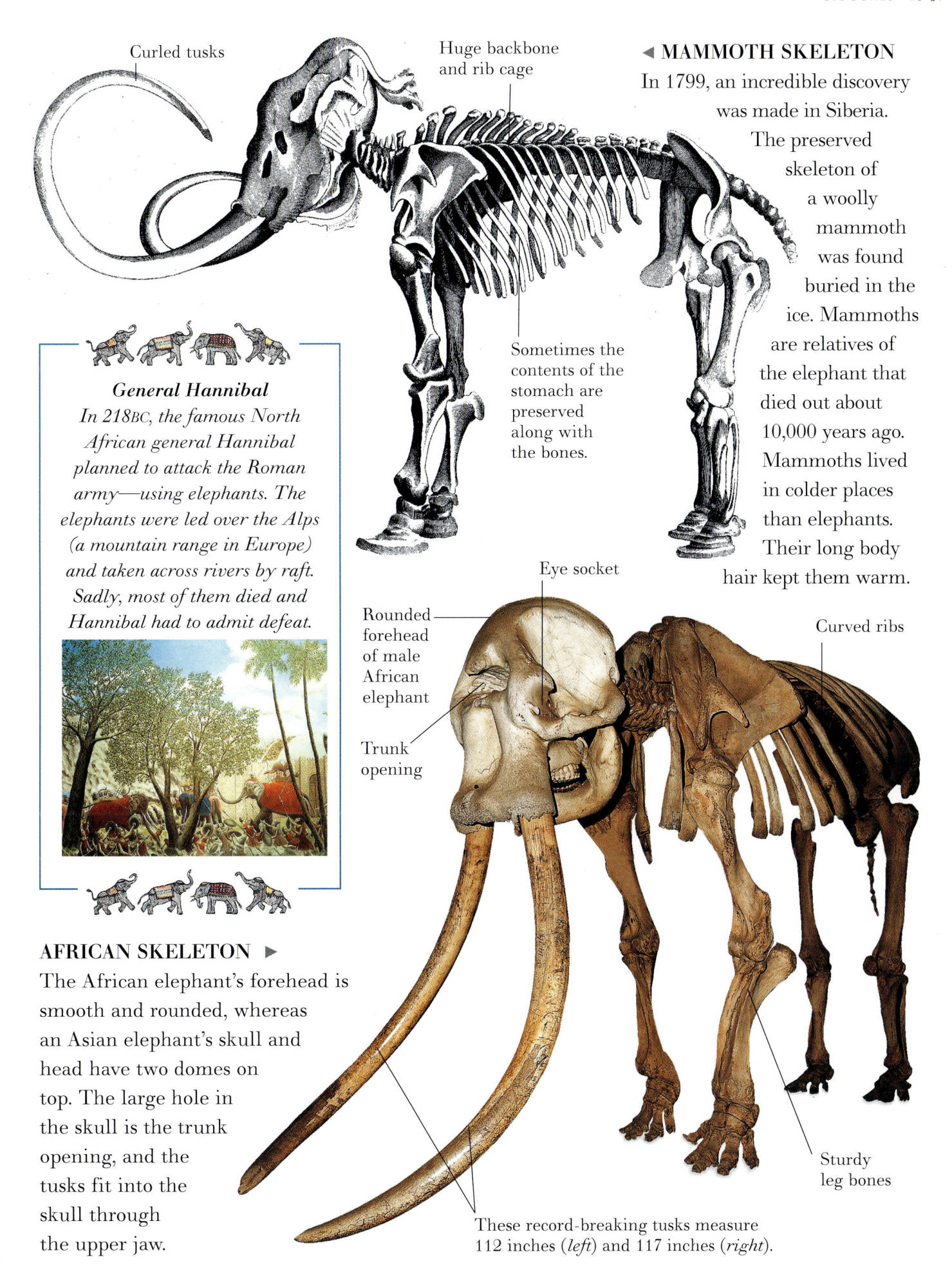

Curled tusks

Huge backbone and rib cage

◄ **MAMMOTH SKELETON**
In 1799, an incredible discovery was made in Siberia. The preserved skeleton of a woolly mammoth was found buried in the ice. Mammoths are relatives of the elephant that died out about 10,000 years ago. Mammoths lived in colder places than elephants. Their long body hair kept them warm.

Sometimes the contents of the stomach are preserved along with the bones.

General Hannibal
In 218BC, the famous North African general Hannibal planned to attack the Roman army—using elephants. The elephants were led over the Alps (a mountain range in Europe) and taken across rivers by raft. Sadly, most of them died and Hannibal had to admit defeat.

Eye socket

Rounded forehead of male African elephant

Curved ribs

Trunk opening

AFRICAN SKELETON ►
The African elephant's forehead is smooth and rounded, whereas an Asian elephant's skull and head have two domes on top. The large hole in the skull is the trunk opening, and the tusks fit into the skull through the upper jaw.

Sturdy leg bones

These record-breaking tusks measure 112 inches (*left*) and 117 inches (*right*).

37

The Bear Facts

Bears may look cuddly and appealing, but in reality they are enormously powerful animals. Bears are mammals with bodies covered in thick fur. They are heavily built with a short tail and large claws. All bears are basically carnivores (meat-eaters), but most enjoy a very mixed diet with just the occasional snack of meat. The exception is the polar bear, which feasts on the blubber (fat) of seals. There are eight species (kinds) of bear: the brown or grizzly bear, American black bear, Asiatic black bear, polar bear, sun bear, sloth bear, spectacled bear, and giant panda. They live in both cold and tropical regions of the world. The sun bears of Southeast Asia are the smallest at 5 feet long, while Alaska's brown bears are the largest at nearly 9 feet long.

Winnie-the-Pooh
The lovable teddy bear Winnie-the-Pooh was created by A.A. Milne. Like real bears, he loves honey. Teddy bears became popular as toys in the early 1900s. President Teddy Roosevelt refused to shoot a bear cub on a hunting trip. Toy bears went on sale soon afterward, known as "Teddy's bears."

◀ BEAR FACE
The brown bear shares the huge dog-like head and face of all bears. Bears have prominent noses, but relatively small eyes and ears. This is because they mostly rely on their sense of smell to help them find food.

▲ BIG FLAT FEET
A polar bear's feet are broad, flat, and furry. The five long, curved claws cannot be retracted (pulled back). One swipe could kill a seal.

Thick fur covers a heavily built body.

A bear's main strength is in its massive shoulders and front legs.

Its broad, flat feet have long claws.

◀ **POINTS OF A BEAR**

The brown bear is called the grizzly bear in North America. Fully-grown brown bears weigh about half a ton. They fear no other animals apart from humans. They can chase prey at high speed, but they rarely bother as they feed mainly on plants.

A bear has a large head, with small eyes and erect, rounded ears.

The long, prominent, dog-like snout dominates the face.

▲ **GIANT PANDA**

China's giant panda, with its distinctive black and white face, is a very unusual bear. Unlike most other bears, which will eat anything, pandas feed almost exclusively on the bamboo plant.

◀ **ARCTIC NOMAD**

Most bears lead a solitary life. The polar bear wanders alone across the Arctic sea ice. Usually it will not tolerate other bears. The exceptions are bears that congregate at rubbish dumps, or mothers accompanied by their cubs, as shown here.

Bear Bodies

Bears are the bully-boys of the animal kingdom, using their size, strength, and deep roar to scare off other animals. Most species (kinds) can stand up on their back legs for a short time to make themselves look even more fierce. At other times, a bear will put its powerful forelimbs to good use in digging, climbing, fishing, and fighting. Bears do not like each other's company and will often attack other bears that cross their path. During fights, bears can do considerable damage with their teeth and claws and survive by sheer brute force. Male bears are generally much larger than females of the same species.

▲ **CLAWS DOWN**
The sun bear has particularly large, curved claws for climbing trees. It spends most of the day sleeping or sunbathing in the branches. At night it strips off bark with its claws, looking for insects and honey in bees' nests.

◄ **PUTTING ON WEIGHT**
This grizzly bear is at peak size. Most bears change size as the seasons pass. They are large and well-fed in the fall, ready for their winter hibernation. When they emerge in spring, they are scrawny with sagging coats.

Beowulf
An Anglo-Saxon poem tells of the hero Beowulf (bear-wolf). He had the strength of a bear and went through many heroic adventures. Beowulf is famous for slaying a monster called Grendel. Here, Beowulf as an old man lies dying from the wounds inflicted by a fire-breathing dragon.

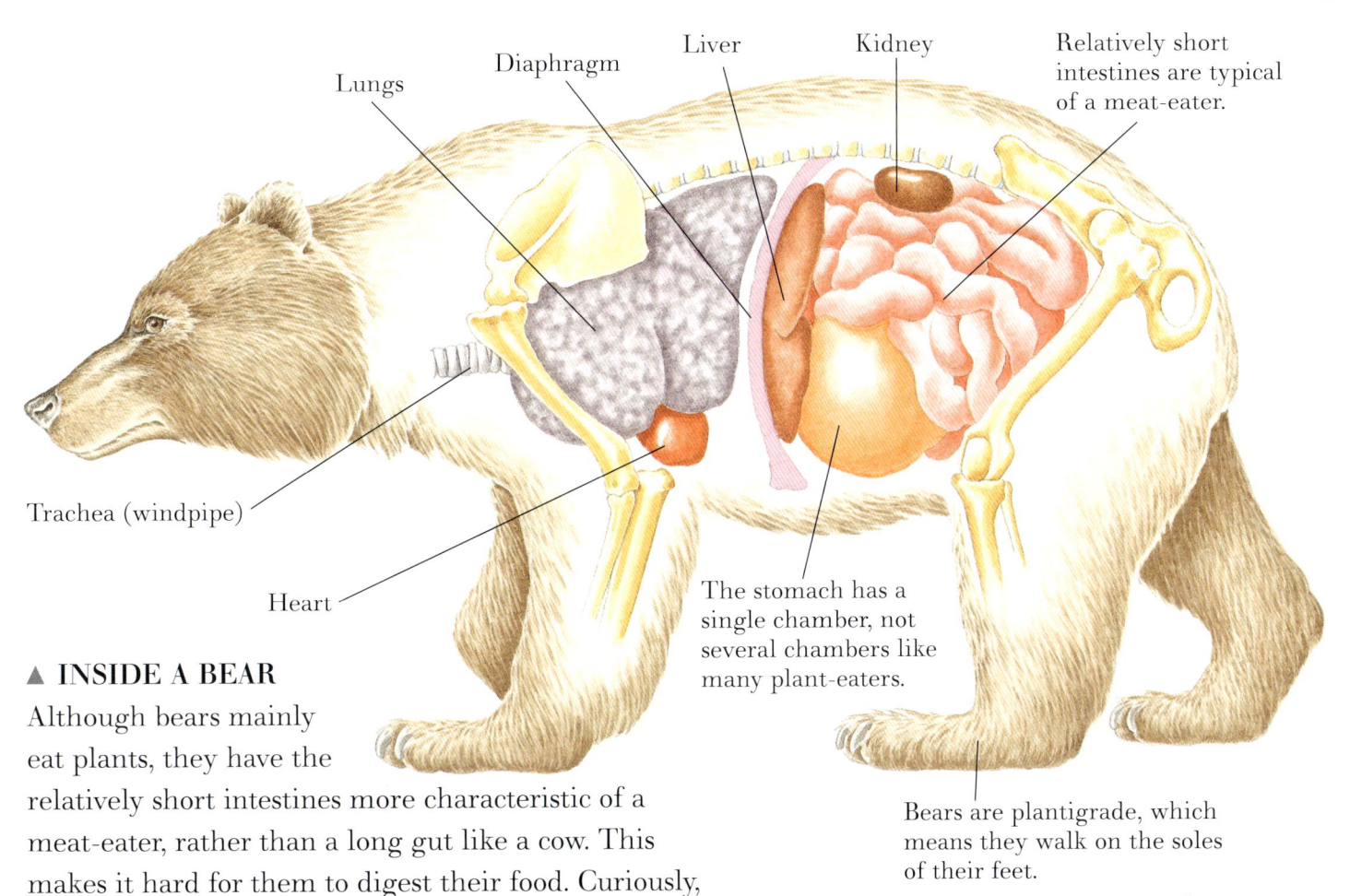

Lungs
Diaphragm
Liver
Kidney
Relatively short intestines are typical of a meat-eater.

Trachea (windpipe)

Heart

The stomach has a single chamber, not several chambers like many plant-eaters.

Bears are plantigrade, which means they walk on the soles of their feet.

▲ INSIDE A BEAR

Although bears mainly eat plants, they have the relatively short intestines more characteristic of a meat-eater, rather than a long gut like a cow. This makes it hard for them to digest their food. Curiously, the bamboo-eating giant panda has the shortest gut of all. Therefore it can digest no more than 20 percent of what it eats, compared to 60 percent in a cow.

▲ SHORT BURSTS

Bears are not particularly agile and swift, but they can run fast over short distances. The brown bear can charge at 31 miles per hour (lions reach about 40 miles per hour) and does sometimes chase its food. A bear at full charge is a frightening sight.

▲ SWEET TOOTH

The sun bear's long slender tongue is ideal for licking honey from bees' nests and for scooping up termites and other insects. Like all bears, it has mobile lips, a flexible snout, and strong jaws.

41

Stealthy Hunters

Cats are native to every continent except Australia and Antarctica. They are mammals with fine fur that is often beautifully marked. All cats are meat-eaters, being skilled hunters and killers with strong agile bodies, acute senses, and sharp teeth and claws. Cats are stealthy and intelligent animals, and most kinds live alone and are very secretive. Although cats vary in size from the domestic (house) cats kept by people as pets to the huge Siberian tiger, both wild and domestic cats share many features and behave in very similar ways. In all, there are 38 different species (kinds) of cat.

▲ LONG TAIL
A cat's long tail helps it to balance as it runs. Cats also use their tails to signal their feelings to other cats.

Only male lions have manes—hairy heads and necks.

Whiskers help a cat feel its surroundings.

The body of a cat is muscular and supple, with a broad, powerful chest.

▲ BIG BITE
As this tiger yawns, it reveals its sharp teeth and strong jaws which can give a lethal bite. Cats use these long canine teeth for killing prey.

▲ PRIDE KING
Unlike other cats, most lions live in groups called prides. Each pride is ruled by a single, large, adult male. The other adult members are all lionesses (females). The lionesses hunt as a team, usually at dusk. Most lions live in the grasslands of Africa, where they feed on large antelopes, such as wildebeests and gazelles.

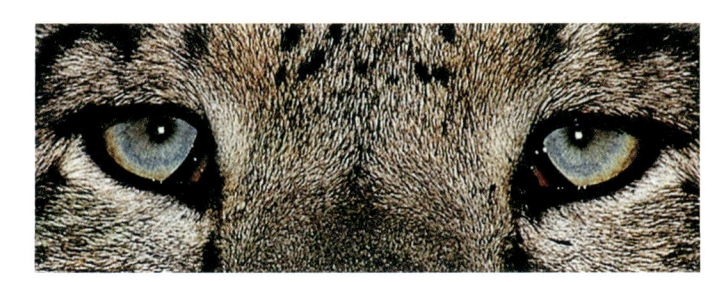

▲ NIGHT SIGHT

The pupils (dark centers) of cats' eyes close to a slit or small circle during the day to keep out the glare. At night they open up to let in as much light as possible. This enables a cat to see clearly at night as well as during the day.

The Lion and the Saint

St Jerome was a Christian scholar who lived from about AD331 to 420. According to legend, he found an injured lion in the desert with a thorn in its paw. Instead of attacking him, the lion befriended the saint when he removed the thorn. St Jerome is often shown with a lion sitting at his feet.

Very soft fur is kept clean by regular grooming with the tongue and paws.

A cat's long tail helps it to balance when leaping on prey.

Cats walk on their toes, not on the whole foot.

Did you know? Some Arctic cultures believe that cats represent the spirits of the dead.

Large ears draw in sounds.

CAT'S EARS ▶

A cat's ears are set high on its head. This gives a keen hunter the best possible chance of picking up sounds. Cats can also swivel their ears to pick up sounds from almost any direction.

Inside a Cat

The skeleton of a cat gives it its shape and has about 230 bones (a human has 206). A cat's short and round skull is joined to the backbone (spine), which supports the body. Vertebrae (bones of the spine) protect the spinal cord, which is the main nerve cable in the body. The ribs are joined to the spine, forming a cage that protects a cat's heart and lungs. Cats' teeth are designed for killing and chewing. Wild cats have to be very careful not to damage their teeth, because with broken teeth they would quickly die from starvation.

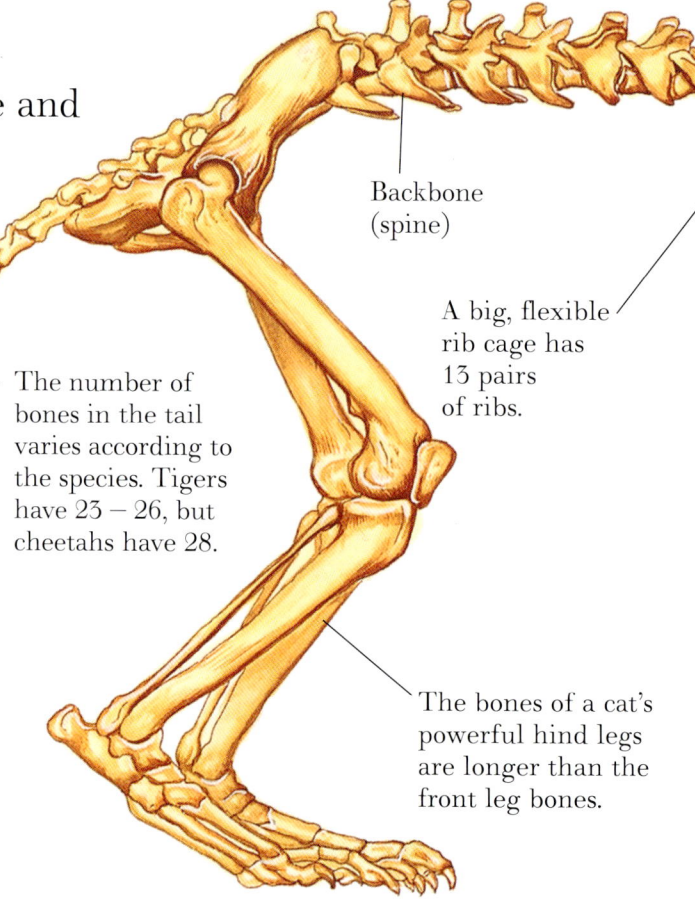

Backbone (spine)

A big, flexible rib cage has 13 pairs of ribs.

The number of bones in the tail varies according to the species. Tigers have 23 – 26, but cheetahs have 28.

The bones of a cat's powerful hind legs are longer than the front leg bones.

▲ THE FRAME

The powerfully built skeleton of a tiger is similar to all cats' skeletons. Cats have short necks with seven compressed vertebrae. These help to streamline and balance the cat so that it can run at great speeds. All cats have slightly different shoulder bones. A cheetah has long shoulder bones to which sprinting muscles are attached. A leopard, however, has short shoulder bones and thicker, tree-climbing muscles.

◄ CANINES AND CARNASSIALS

A tiger reveals its fearsome teeth. Its long, curved canines are adapted to fit between the neck bones of its prey to break the spinal cord. Like all carnivores, cats have strong back teeth, called carnassials. These teeth work like scissors, slicing through meat.

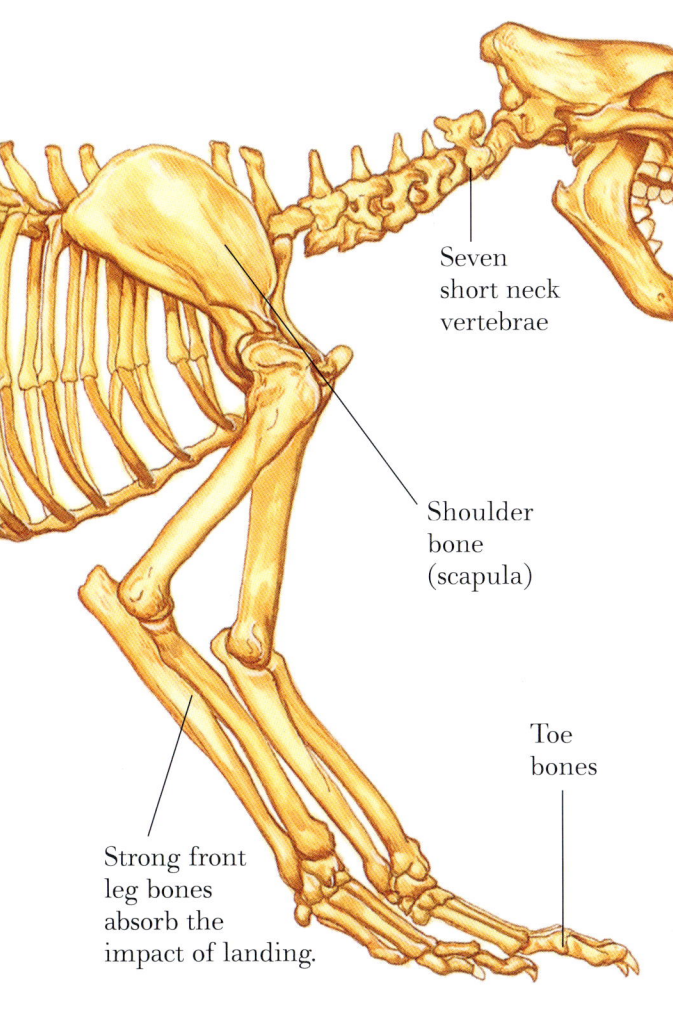

Seven short neck vertebrae

Shoulder bone (scapula)

Toe bones

Strong front leg bones absorb the impact of landing.

LANDING FEET ▶
As it falls, this cat twists its supple, flexible spine to make sure its feet will be in the right place for landing. Cats almost always land on their feet when they fall. This helps them to avoid injury as they leap on prey or jump from a tree.

▼ CHEWING ON A BONE
Ravenous lions feast on the carcass of their latest kill. Cats' jaws are hinged so that their jaw bones can move only up and down. Because of this, cats eat on one side of their mouths at a time and they often tilt their heads when they eat.

▼ CAT SKULL
Like all cats' skulls, this tiger's skull has a high crown at the back giving lots of space for the attachment of its strong neck muscles. The eye sockets hold large eyes that let it see well to the sides as well as to the front. Its short jaws can open wide to deliver a powerful bite.

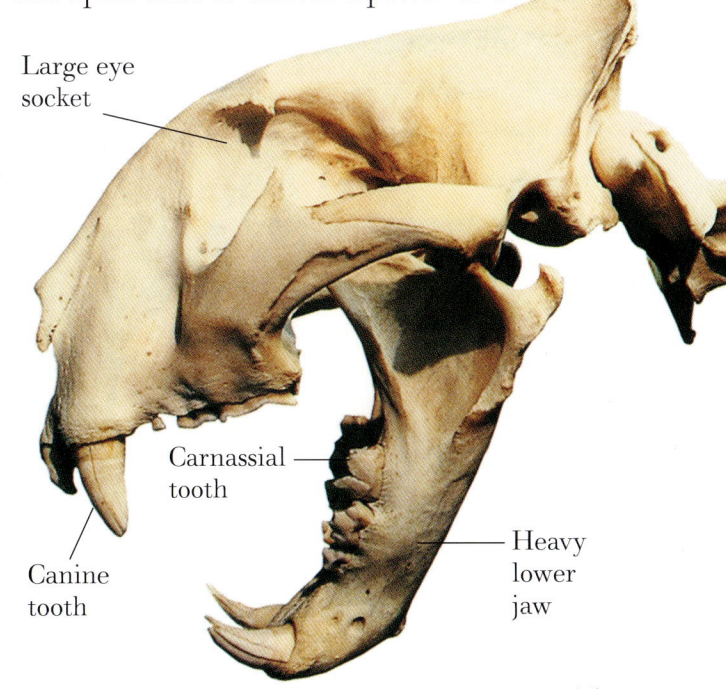

Large eye socket

Carnassial tooth

Canine tooth

Heavy lower jaw

45

Killing Machines

Both inside and out, cats are designed to be killers. Thick back and shoulder muscles make them powerful jumpers and climbers. Long, dagger-like teeth and sharp, curved claws that grow from all of their digits (toes) are their weapons. One of the digits on a cat's front foot is called the dew claw. This is held off the ground to keep it sharp and ready to hold prey. Cats are warm-blooded, which means that their bodies stay at the same temperature no matter how hot or cold the weather is. The fur on their skin keeps them warm when conditions are cold. When it is hot, cats cool down by sweating through their noses and paw pads.

Hercules and the Nemean Lion
The mythical Greek hero Hercules was the son of the god Zeus and tremendously strong. As a young man he committed a terrible crime. Part of his punishment was to kill the Nemean lion. The lion had impenetrable skin and could not be killed with arrows or spears. Hercules chased the lion into a cave and strangled it with his hands. He wore its skin as a shield and its head as a helmet.

▼ KNOCKOUT CLAWS

Cheetahs have well-developed dew claws that stick out from their front legs. They use these claws to knock down prey before grabbing its throat or muzzle to finish it off. Other cats use their dew claws to grip while climbing or to hold onto prey. Cats have five claws, including the dew claw, on their front paws. On their back paws, they have only four claws.

Did you know? Cats cannot digest sugar so they prefer not to eat sweet things.

Dew claw —

Dew claw ——

46

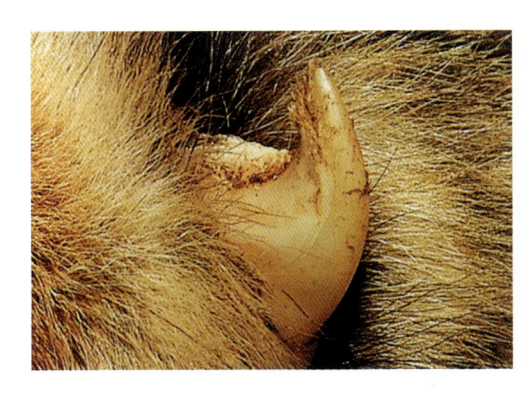

▲ TIGER CLAW
This is the extended claw of a tiger. Cats' claws are made of keratin, just like human fingernails. They need to be kept sharp all the time.

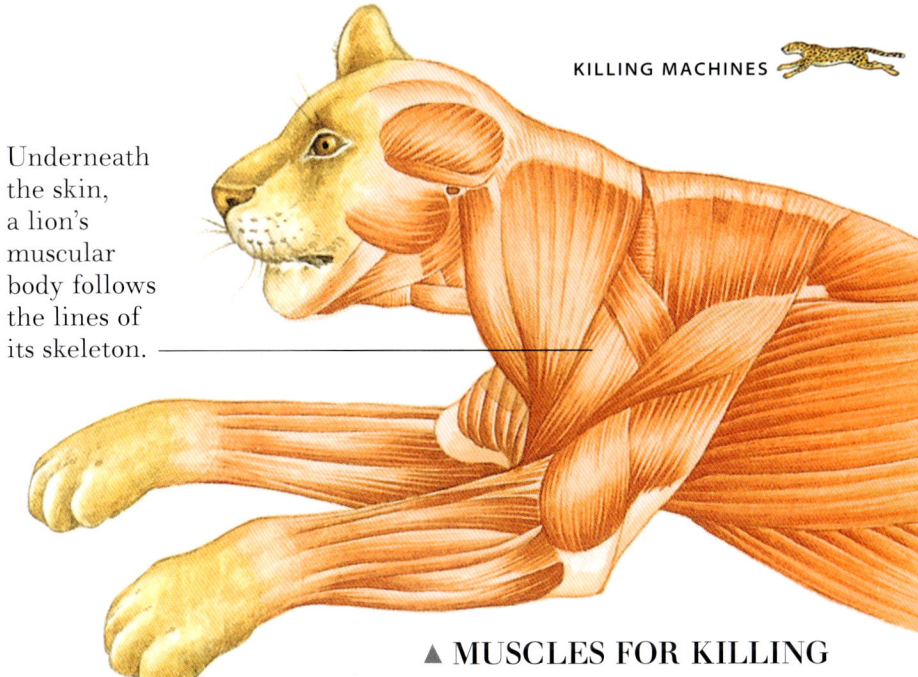

Underneath the skin, a lion's muscular body follows the lines of its skeleton.

▲ MUSCLES FOR KILLING
Cats have very strong shoulder and neck muscles which give it power to attack prey. The muscles also absorb some of the impact when the cat pounces.

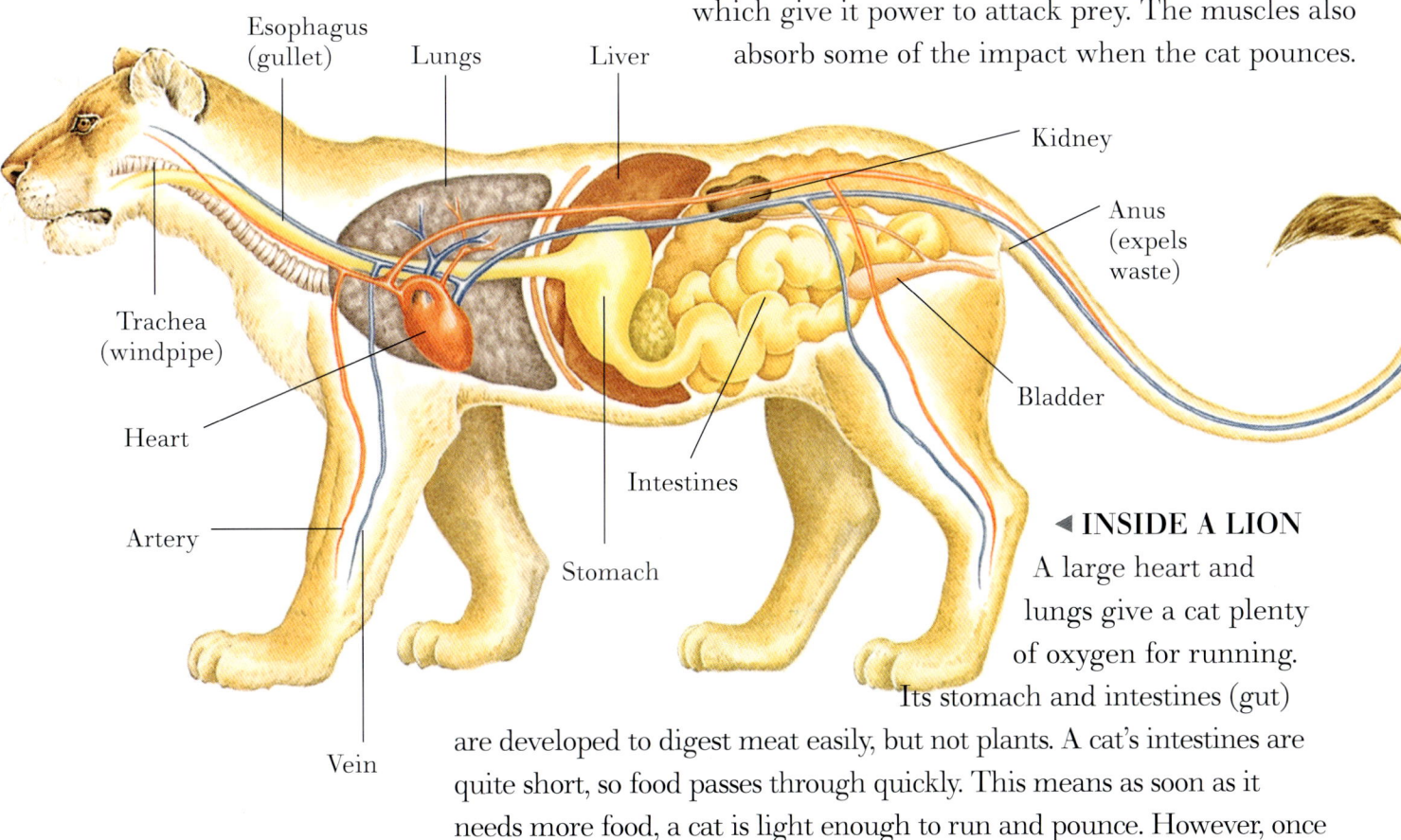

Esophagus (gullet)

Lungs

Liver

Kidney

Anus (expels waste)

Trachea (windpipe)

Heart

Artery

Intestines

Stomach

Bladder

Vein

◄ INSIDE A LION
A large heart and lungs give a cat plenty of oxygen for running. Its stomach and intestines (gut) are developed to digest meat easily, but not plants. A cat's intestines are quite short, so food passes through quickly. This means as soon as it needs more food, a cat is light enough to run and pounce. However, once a lion has had a big meal, it does not need to eat again for several days.

CLAW PROTECTION ►
Cats retract (pull back) their claws into fleshy sheaths to protect them. This prevents them from getting blunt or damaged. Only cheetahs do not have sheaths.

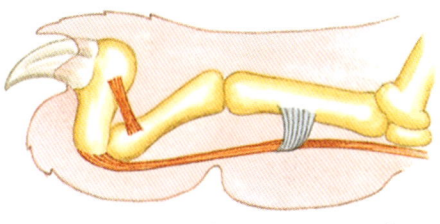

Sheathed claw is protected by a fleshy covering.

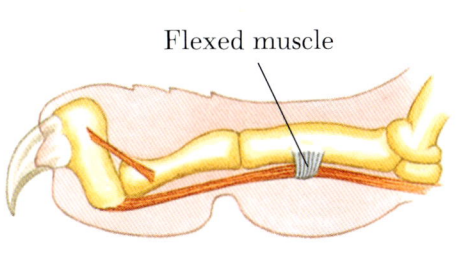

Flexed muscle

The claw is unsheathed when a muscle tightens.

Running Wild

Wolves are wild members of the dog family (canids). They have gleaming yellow eyes and lean, muscular bodies. The 37 different species (kinds) of canids include jackals, coyotes, foxes, and wild and domestic dogs, as well as wolves. Canids are native to every continent except Australia and Antarctica. All of them share a keen sense of smell and hearing, and are carnivores (meat-eaters). Wolves and wild dogs hunt live prey, which they kill with their sharp teeth. However, many canids also eat vegetable matter and even insects. They are among the most intelligent of all animals. Many, including the wolves, are highly social animals that live together in groups called packs.

Large, triangular ears, usually held pricked (erect)

Powerful shoulders and supple body

BODY FEATURES ▶
The wolf is the largest wild dog. It has a strong, well-muscled body covered with dense, shaggy fur, a long, bushy tail, and strong legs made for running. Its muzzle (nose and jaws) is long and well developed and its ears are large. Male and female wolves look very similar, although females are generally the smaller of the two.

▲ PRODUCING YOUNG
A female wolf suckles (feeds) her cubs. All canids are mammals and feed their young on milk. Females produce a litter of cubs, or pups, once a year. Most are born in an underground den.

48

◄ KEEN SENSES

The jackal, like all dogs, has very keen senses. Its nose can detect faint scents and its large ears pick up the slightest sound. Smell and hearing are mainly used for hunting. Many canids also have good vision.

Thick, coarse fur helps to protect the wolf from extremes of temperature.

Long, bushy tail

Strong, powerful, muscular legs

Canids walk on all fours on the pads of their toes.

The Big, Bad Wolf

Fairy tales often depict wolves as wicked, dangerous animals. In the tale of the Three Little Pigs, the big, bad wolf terrorizes three small pigs. Eventually he is outwitted by the smartest pig, who builds a brick house that the wolf cannot blow down, and all the pigs are safe.

▲ LIVING IN PACKS

Wolves and many other wild dogs live in groups called packs of about eight to 20. Each pack has a hierarchy (social order) and is led by the strongest male and female.

EXPERT HUNTERS ►

A wolf bares its teeth in a snarl to defend its kill. Wolves and other canids feed mainly on meat, but eat plants, too, particularly when they are hungry.

Body of a Wild Dog

Muscular, fast-running wolves and wild dogs are built for chasing prey in open country. Thick muscles and long, strong legs enable them to run fast over great distances. The long muzzle helps the wolf to seize prey on the run. The wolf has a large stomach that can digest meat quickly and hold a big meal after a successful hunt. Wolves, however, can also go without food for more than a week if prey is scarce. Teeth are a wolf's main weapon, used for biting enemies, catching prey, and tearing food. Small incisors (front teeth) strip flesh off bones. Long fangs (canines) grab and hold prey. Toward the back, jagged carnassial teeth close together like shears to slice meat into small pieces, while large molars can crush bones.

◄ **POWERFUL MUSCLES**

The muscles in the neck, shoulders, and hindquarters of wolves and other canids are very well developed. These give the wolf strength and long-distance stamina as well as speed. When hunting, a wolf pack chases its prey, such as a large deer, until the victim is totally exhausted. Then the pack bites the animal to death.

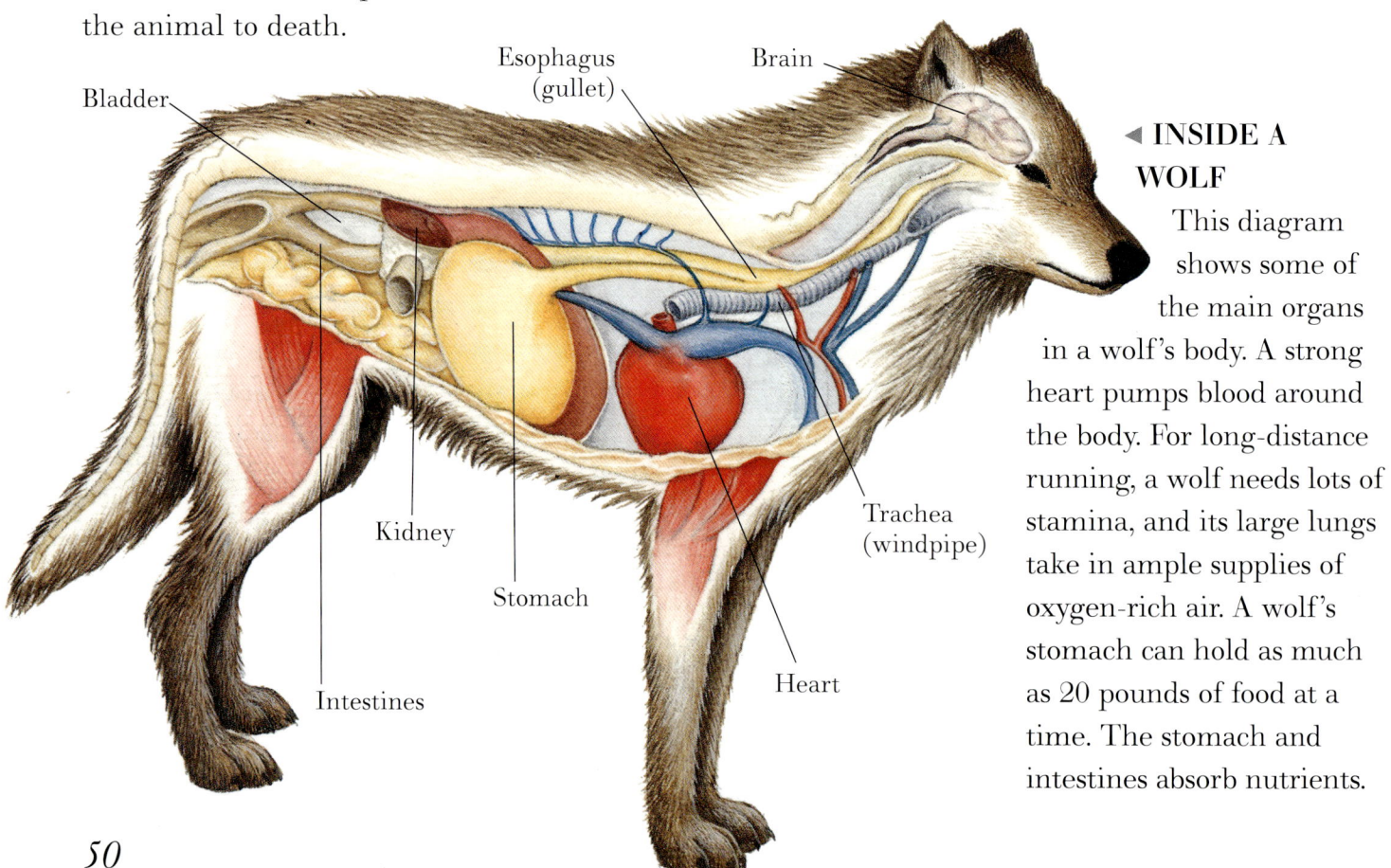

Bladder

Esophagus (gullet)

Brain

Kidney

Stomach

Intestines

Heart

Trachea (windpipe)

◄ **INSIDE A WOLF**

This diagram shows some of the main organs in a wolf's body. A strong heart pumps blood around the body. For long-distance running, a wolf needs lots of stamina, and its large lungs take in ample supplies of oxygen-rich air. A wolf's stomach can hold as much as 20 pounds of food at a time. The stomach and intestines absorb nutrients.

▼ WOLF'S SKULL

A wolf's head has a broad crown and a tapering muzzle. The bones of the skull are strong and heavy. They form a tough case that protects the animal's brain, eyes, ears, and nose. The jaws have powerful muscles that can exert great pressure as the wolf sinks its teeth into its prey.

molar carnassial canine incisor

▼ BAT-EARED FOX SKULL

The bat-eared fox has a delicate, tapering muzzle. Its jaws are weaker than a wolf's and suited to deal with smaller prey, such as insects. This fox has 46–50 teeth, which is more than any other canid. Extra molars at the back of the animal's mouth enable it to crunch insects, such as beetles, which have a tough outer casing on their bodies.

molar carnassial canine incisor

▲ TIME FOR BED

A wolf shows its full set of meat-eating teeth as it yawns. Wolves and most other canids have 42 teeth. In wolves, the four large, dagger-like canines at the front of the mouth can grow up to 2 inches long.

COOLING DOWN ▶

Like all mammals, the wolf is warm-blooded. This means that its body temperature remains constant whatever the weather, so it is always ready to spring into action. Wolves do not have sweat glands all over their bodies as humans do, so in hot weather they cannot sweat to cool down. When the wolf gets too hot, it opens its mouth and pants with its tongue lolling out. Moisture evaporates from the nose, mouth, and tongue to cool the animal down.

Monkey Power

The primates are a group of mammals that include monkeys, apes, and also humans. Many of them have large brains and are among the most intelligent of animals, but their bodies are still largely the same as those of most other mammals. Small primate bodies are built for flexibility and agility, with hinged joints supported by long, elastic muscles to allow maximum range of movement. Body shapes vary according to whether the animals climb and leap through trees or move along the ground. Head shape and size depend on whether brainpower or the sense of smell or sight is top priority.

▲ **DENTAL PRACTICE**
Monkeys and prosimians (monkey relatives) have four types of teeth—incisors for cutting, canines for stabbing and ripping, and molars and premolars for grinding tough leaves and fruit into a paste.

▼ **INTERNAL VIEW**
A monkey's bones and strong muscles protect the vital organs inside its body. Its facial muscles let it make expressions. Monkey legs are generally shorter in relation to their bodies than lemur legs. This gives them more precise climbing and reaching skills, especially in the treetops.

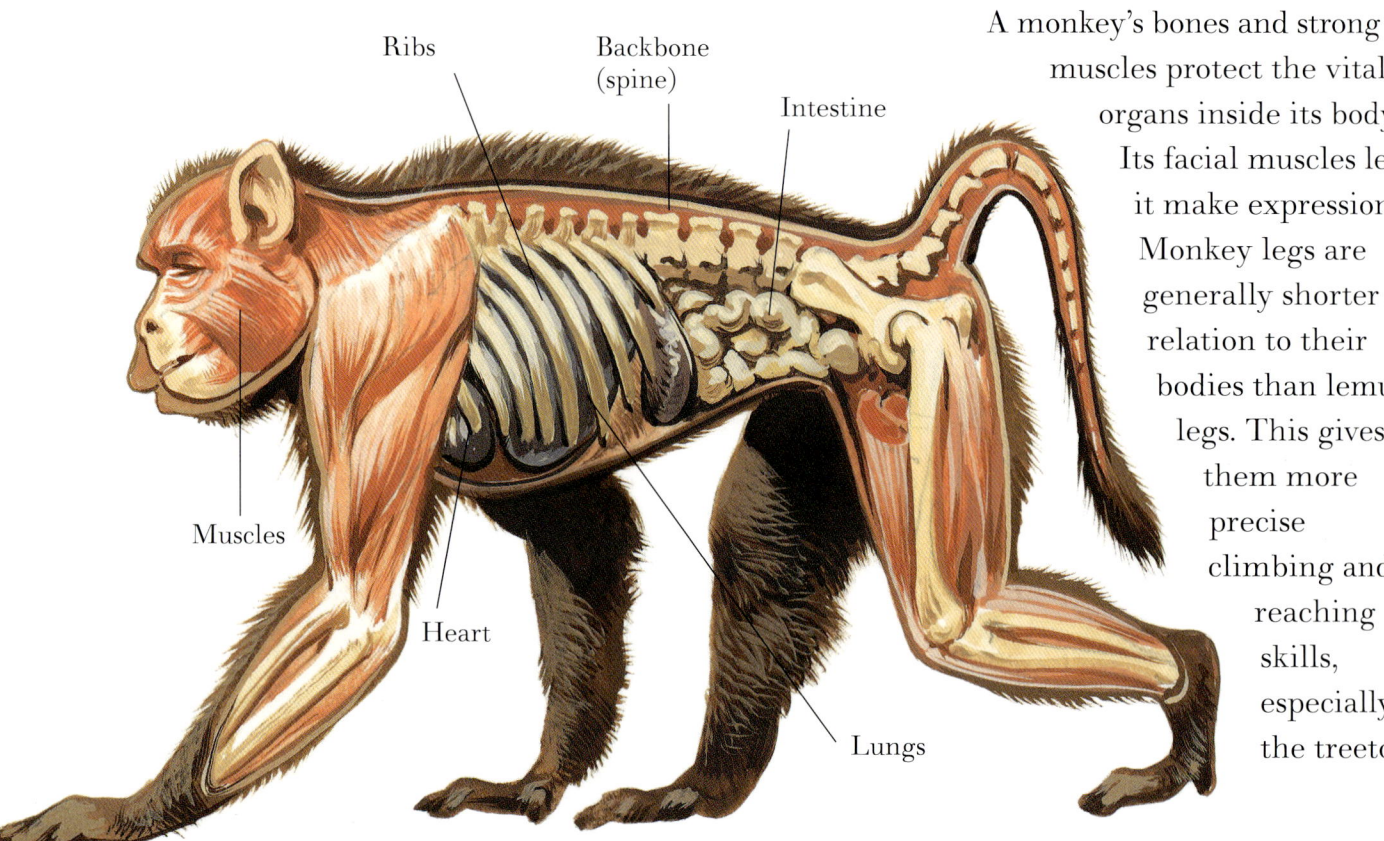

Ribs

Backbone (spine)

Intestine

Muscles

Heart

Lungs

▼ BIG EYES

The tarsier has the biggest eyes of any animal in relation to its body size. There is not much room left in its skull for a brain and each of the eyes is heavier than the brain. Prosimians have simpler lives than monkeys and do not need big brains. Instead, they have an array of sharp senses—more sensitive than monkeys'—that help them to survive. As well as its huge eyes, this tarsier has large ears that pick up the slightest sounds in the quiet of the night.

▲ A STRONG STOMACH

A baboon's digestive system can cope with raw meat as well as plant food. These big monkeys catch and eat rodents, rabbits, and even small antelopes as well as lots of insects. Most monkeys and prosimians eat mainly plants and have relatively large stomachs and long guts because leaves and other plant foods are hard to digest.

INSIDE LOOK AT A LEMUR ▶

Lemurs belong to a group of monkey relatives called prosimians. These are less advanced than the monkeys. This skeleton of a ruffed lemur has a long, narrow head, which has less space for the brain, and its legs are very long compared to the length of its body. Their long legs help lemurs to leap great distances from tree to tree and enable them to cling in a relaxed fashion to vertical tree trunks.

What is a Great Ape?

The four great apes—the chimpanzee, bonobo, gorilla, and orangutan—look similar to us because they are our closest animal relatives. Humans are sometimes called the fifth great ape. Great apes are also closely related to the lesser apes, called gibbons. Nearly 99 per cent of our genes are the same as those of a chimpanzee. In fact, chimpanzees are more closely related to humans than they are to gorillas. Like us, the other great apes are intelligent, use tools, solve problems, and communicate. They can also learn simple language, although their vocal cords cannot produce enough sounds to speak words.

▼ **APE FEATURES**

Gorillas are the largest of the great apes. Typical ape features include long arms (longer than their legs), flexible wrist joints, gripping thumbs and fingers, and no tail. Apes are clever, with big brains.

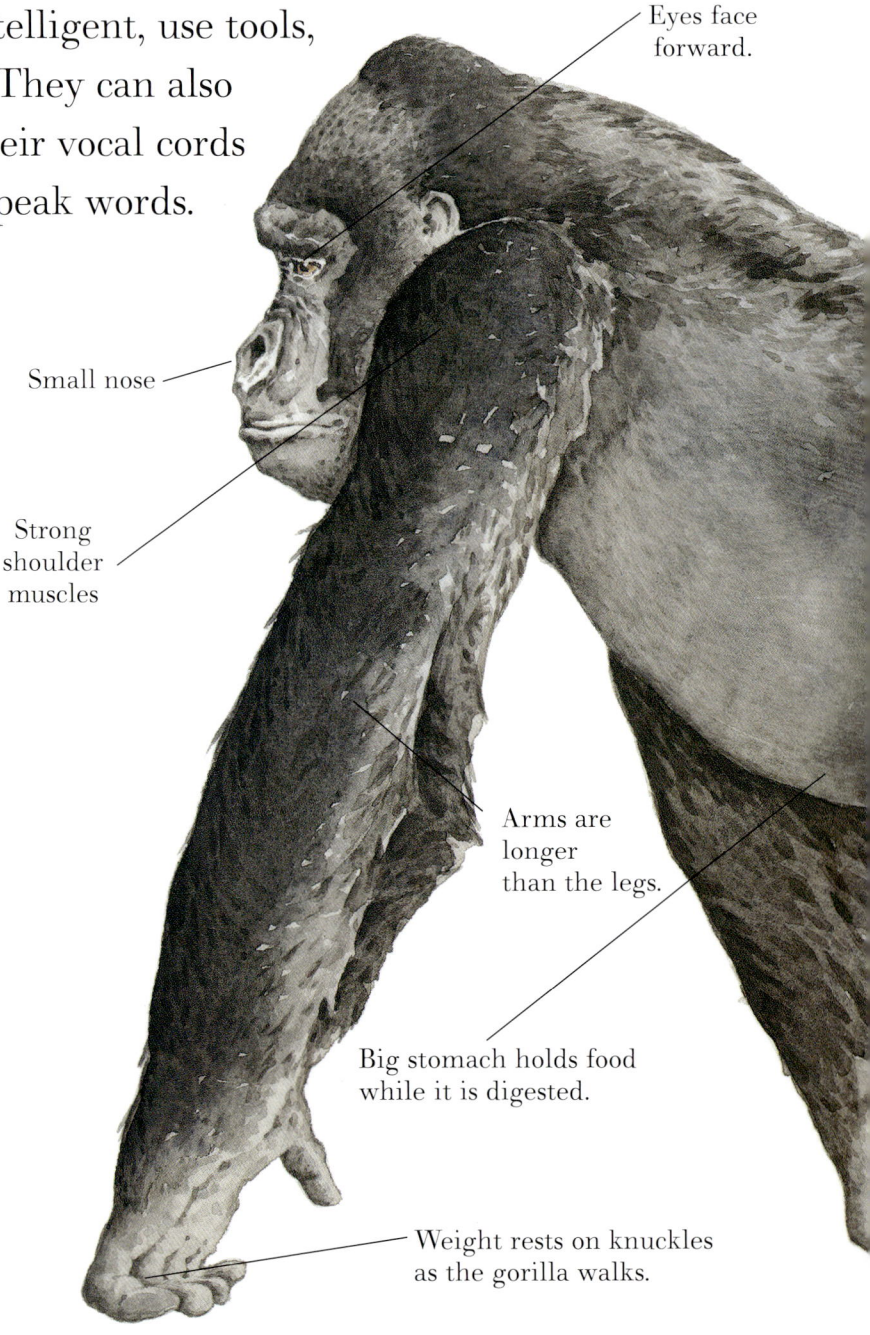

Eyes face forward.

Small nose

Strong shoulder muscles

Arms are longer than the legs.

Big stomach holds food while it is digested.

Weight rests on knuckles as the gorilla walks.

▲ **RED APE**

Red, shaggy orangutans are the largest tree-living animals in the world. Their name means old-man-of-the-forest. Orangutans live on the islands of Borneo and Sumatra in Southeast Asia.

54

▲ STUDYING APES

Much of what we know today about wild apes is based on the work of scientists such as Dr Dian Fossey, who spent many years carefully observing gorillas in the wild.

GROUPS ►

Family groups of between five and 40 gorillas live together in the misty rainforests and mountains of central Africa. Each group is led by an adult male. He decides where the group will feed, sleep, and travel.

Apes do not have a tail.

Feet rest flat on the ground.

King Kong

At the beginning of the 1930s, the film King Kong *showed a giant gorilla as a dangerous monster. In the movie, a team of hunters capture Kong and take him to America. We now know that gorillas are peaceful animals, very different from the movie monster.*

▼ APE FACES

Have you ever watched a chimpanzee in a zoo and found that it has turned to watch you? Great apes are often as interested in watching us as we are in watching them.

Inside a Great Ape

Characteristic features of great apes are their long, strong arms and flexible shoulders, which they use to clamber through the trees. They do not have tails to help them balance and grip the branches. Instead of hooves or paws, apes have hands and feet that can grasp branches and hold food very well. On the ground, an ape's strong arms and fingers take its weight as it walks on all fours. Humans are different from the other apes as they have short arms and long legs. Human arms are about 30 percent shorter than human legs. Our bodies and bones are also designed for walking upright rather than for swinging through the trees. All the apes have a large head, with a big skull inside, to protect an intelligent brain.

◀ **APE SKELETON**
One of the notable features of an ape skeleton is the large skull that surrounds and protects the big brain. Apes also have long, strong finger and toe bones for gripping branches. The arm bones of the orangutans, gorillas, and chimpanzees are also extended, making their arms longer than their legs.

Did you know? Female orangutans can weigh up to 88 pounds but males can weigh over

▼ **THE BIG FIVE**
All great apes have similar bodies, although a human's body is less hairy and muscular than the bodies of the other apes. The main differences between ape bodies lie in the shape of the skull and also the length of the arms and legs. Orangutans have extra-long arms to hang from branches, while humans have long legs for walking upright.

Orangutan   Gorilla   Bonobo   Chimpanzee   Human

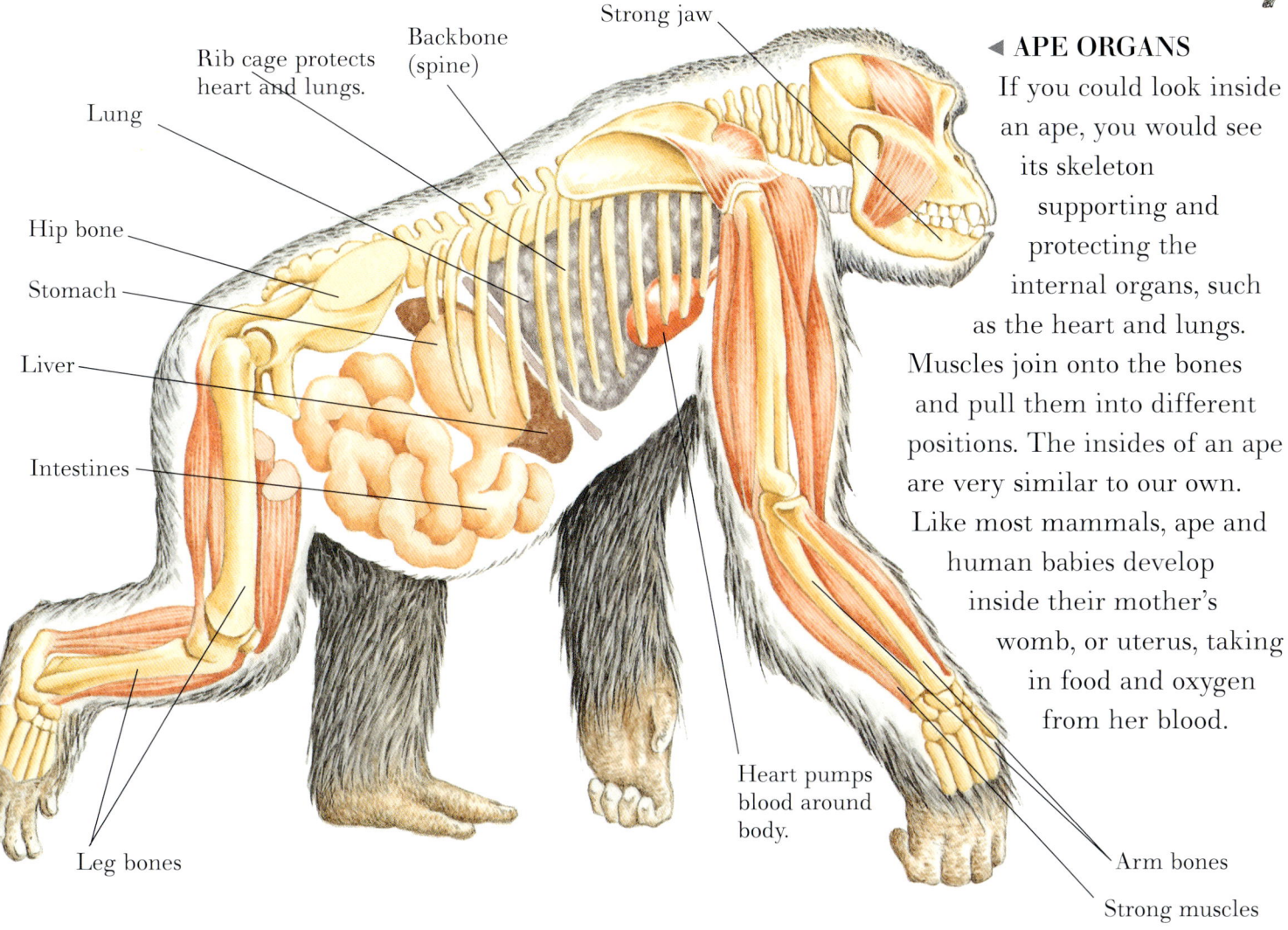

Strong jaw

Backbone
(spine)

Rib cage protects
heart and lungs.

Lung

Hip bone

Stomach

Liver

Intestines

Leg bones

Heart pumps
blood around
body.

Arm bones

Strong muscles

◀ **APE ORGANS**

If you could look inside
an ape, you would see
its skeleton
supporting and
protecting the
internal organs, such
as the heart and lungs.
Muscles join onto the bones
and pull them into different
positions. The insides of an ape
are very similar to our own.
Like most mammals, ape and
human babies develop
inside their mother's
womb, or uterus, taking
in food and oxygen
from her blood.

▲ **NO TAIL**

Apes, such as chimpanzees, do not have
tails, but most monkeys do. Apes
clamber and hang by their powerful
arms. Monkeys walk along branches on
all fours, using the tail for balance.

EXTRA HAND ▶

Unlike the apes,
monkeys that live
in the dense
rainforests of
Central and South
America have
special gripping
tails, called
prehensile tails.
The tails also have
sensitive tips that
work like an extra
one-fingered
hand, letting the
apes cling to
the branches when
gathering fruit.

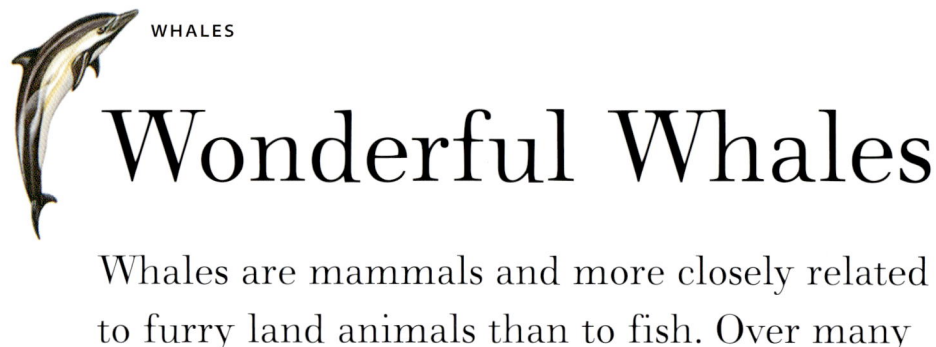

Wonderful Whales

Whales are mammals and more closely related to furry land animals than to fish. Over many millions of years, whales have developed features that suit them to a life spent mostly underwater. They have long, rounded bodies and smooth, almost hairless skin. There are two types of whale: toothed whales, such as dolphins, feed on fish, while baleen whales strain smaller creatures from seawater.

▼ BIG MOUTH

This gray whale is a baleen whale. Its baleen—drapes of fine plates—can be seen hanging from its upper jaw. The whale filters food from gulps of seawater by straining it through gaps between the plates of the baleen. Baleen whales have large mouths to take in a lot of water.

Baleen

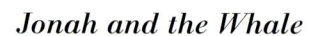

Jonah and the Whale

This picture from the 17th century tells one of the best known of all Bible stories. The prophet Jonah was thrown overboard by sailors during a terrible storm. To rescue him, God sent a whale, which swallowed him whole. Jonah spent three days in the whale's belly before it coughed him up onto dry land. The picture shows that many people at this time had little idea of what a whale looked like. The artist has given it shark-like teeth and a curly tail.

▼ LEAPING DOLPHINS

A pair of bottlenose dolphins leap effortlessly several feet out of the water. Powerful muscles near the tail provide them with the energy for fast swimming and leaping. They leap for various reasons—to signal to each other, to look for fish, or perhaps just for fun.

▲ HANGERS ON

This humpback whale's throat is covered with barnacles, which take hold because the whale moves quite slowly. They cannot easily cling to swifter-moving whales, such as dolphins. A dolphin sheds rough skin as it moves through the water. This also makes it harder for a barnacle to take hold.

LOUSY WHALES ▶

The gray whale's skin is covered with light-colored patches. These patches are clusters of ten-legged lice, called cyamids, which are ¾–1¼ inches long. They feed on the whale's skin.

◀ BODY LINES

A pod, or group, of melon-headed whales swim in the Pacific Ocean. This species is one of the smaller whales, at less than 10 feet long. It shows the features of a typical whale—a well-rounded body with a short neck and a single fin on the back. It has a pair of paddle-like front flippers and a tail with horizontal flukes.

Did you know? Whales have whiskers on their faces.

59

Shark Attack

Sharks are perfect underwater killing machines. All sharks are fish, related to rays and dogfish. Unlike most other fish, sharks do not have bones. Instead their bodies are supported by springy cartilage. Although most sharks are cold-blooded—their bodies are always the same temperature as the seawater—some sharks, such as the great white and mako, can keep their bodies warmer than the water around them. Warm bodies are more efficient, letting the sharks swim faster. Sharks have a huge, oil-filled liver that helps to keep them afloat. However, most ocean sharks must swim all the time. If they were to stop, not only would they sink, but they would also be unable to breathe. Some sharks can take a rest on the seabed by pumping water over their gills to breathe.

▲ **GILL BREATHERS**
Like almost all fish, this sixgill shark breathes by taking oxygen-rich water into its mouth. The oxygen passes through the gills into the blood, and the water leaves through the gill slits.

▲ **OCEAN RACER**
The shortfin mako shark is the fastest shark in the sea. Using special, warm muscles, it can travel at speeds of 22–31 miles per hour. It uses its speed to catch fast-swimming swordfish.

◀ **SUSPENDED ANIMATION**
The sandtiger shark can hold air in its stomach. The air acts like a life preserver, helping the shark to hover in the water. Sandtiger sharks stay afloat without moving, lurking among rocks and caves as they wait for shoals of fish.

KEEP MOVING ►

Like many hunting sharks, the gray reef shark cannot breathe unless it moves forward. The forward motion pushes water over its gills. If it stops moving, the shark will drown. Sharks have to swim even when they are asleep.

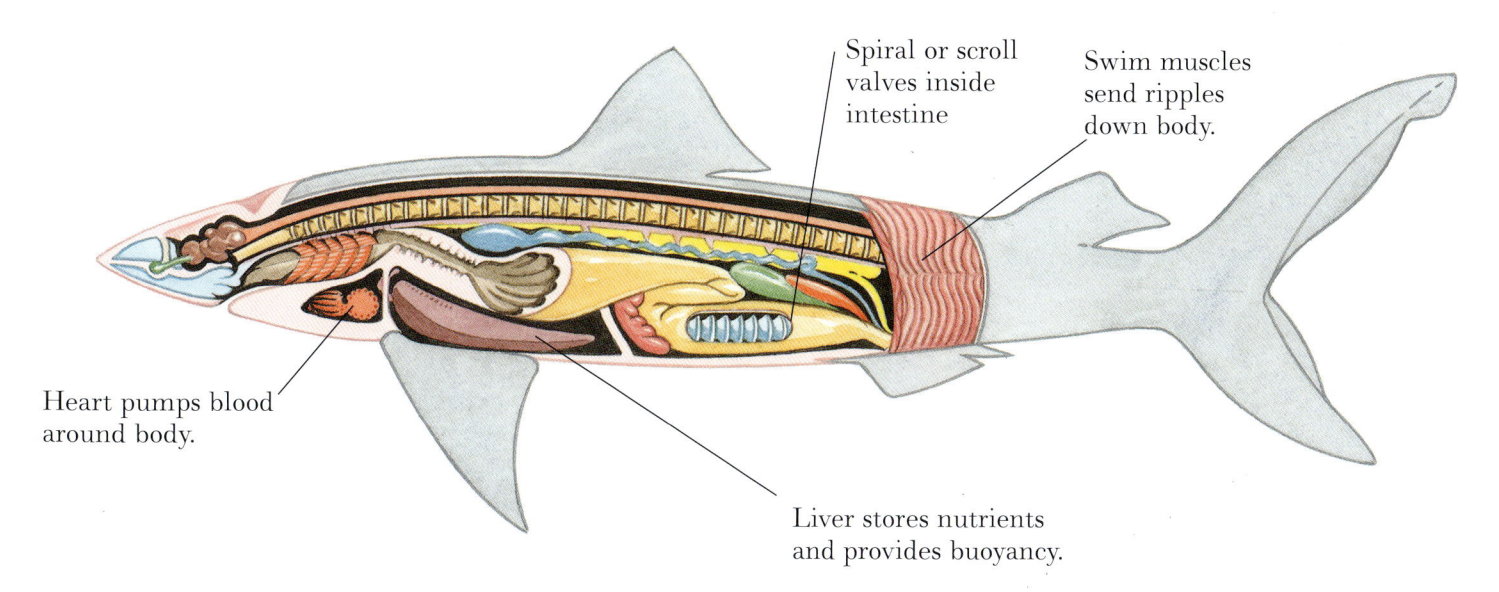

Spiral or scroll valves inside intestine

Swim muscles send ripples down body.

Heart pumps blood around body.

Liver stores nutrients and provides buoyancy.

▲ INSIDE A SHARK

A shark has thick muscles, a spiral or scroll valve in the intestine, which increases the area for absorbing digested food. It also has blood vessels that carry oxygen from the gills around the body.

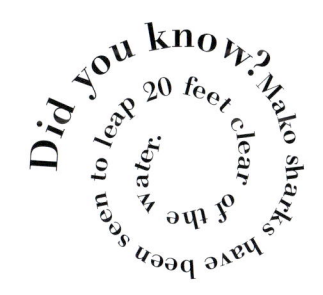

Did you know? Mako sharks have been seen to leap 20 feet clear of the water.

◄ ABLE TO REST

The tawny nurse shark pumps water over its gills by lifting the floor of its mouth. This lets it rest on the seabed, yet still breathe. Whitetip reef sharks, lemon sharks, catsharks, and nursehounds also do this.

Glossary

abdomen
The rear section of an animal's body that holds the reproductive organs and part of the animal's digestive system.

antenna (pl antennae)
The long projections on an insect's head, which it uses to smell, touch, and taste.

artery
A blood vessel that carries blood away from the heart.

arthropod
An animal without a backbone that has many jointed legs and an exoskeleton on the outside of its body. Arthropods include spiders, insects, crabs, and woodlice.

bladder
Where waste urine is stored in the body before being expelled.

canine
A sharp, pointed tooth that grips and pierces the skin of prey.

carnivore
An animal that feeds on the flesh of other animals.

cloaca
A chamber at the very rear of the gut in fish, amphibians, reptiles, and birds. The reproductive and urinary systems open into it.

cold-blooded
An animal whose temperature varies according to its surroundings.

crocodilian
A member of the group of animals that includes crocodiles, alligators, gharials, and caimans.

diaphragm
A sheet of muscle separating the chest cavity from the abdominal cavity of mammals. Its movement helps with breathing.

digestion
The process by which food is broken down so that it can be absorbed by the body.

environment
The conditions of an area an animal lives in.

equids
Horses and horse-like animals, such as asses.

esophagus
Part of the gut of an animal, usually long and tube-shaped. It transports swallowed food from the mouth to the stomach.

exoskeleton
The hard outer layer of an insect that protects the soft parts inside.

feral
Domestic animals that have escaped or been abandoned and are now living freely in the wild.

gene/genetics
The code for a physical trait and the way this is passed from one generation to another. Each gene contains a strand of DNA that is responsible for a feature, such as blue eyes.

gill
Part of an animal's body used for breathing underwater.

herbivore
An animal that eats only plants.

hibernation
A period of sleep during the winter when body processes slow down. Animals, such as bears hibernate mainly because food is scarce and they might starve otherwise.

incisor teeth
Sharp teeth in the front of a mammal's mouth that are used for biting and nibbling food.

insect
An invertebrate (no backbone) animal which has three body parts, six legs, and usually two pairs of wings. Beetles, bugs, and butterflies are all insects.

intestine
Part of an animal's gut where food is broken down and absorbed.

joint
The point of contact between two bones, this also includes the ligaments that join them.

Latin name
The scientific name for a species. An animal often has many different common names throughout the world. The Latin name prevents confusion because it never alters.

liver
An organ that processes food from the digestive system (gut). One of the liver's main tasks is to remove any poisons from the blood.

lung
An organ of the body that takes in oxygen from the air.

mammal
A warm-blooded animal with a backbone. Most have hair or fur. Mammals feed their offspring on milk from the mother's body.

migration
A regular journey some animals make from one habitat to another, because of changes in the weather or their food supply, or to breed.

minibeasts
Small creatures such as insects, spiders and centipedes.

molar
A broad, ridged tooth in the back of a mammal's jaw, used for grinding up food.

muscle
An animal tissue made up of bundles of cells that can contract (shorten) to produce movement.

organ
A part of the body or plant which has a special function, e.g. a kidney in the body, a leaf in a plant.

palps
Short stalks that project from the mouthparts of a butterfly, moth, or spider which act as sensors.

predator
An animal that hunts and kills other animals for food.

prey
An animal that is hunted by other animals for food.

raptor
Any bird of prey. From the Latin *rapere* meaning to seize, grasp, or take by force.

regurgitate
To bring up food that has already been swallowed.

saliva
A colourless liquid that is produced by glands in the mouth.

skeleton
The framework of bones that supports and often protects the body of an animal and to which the muscles are usually attached.

spiracles
The holes in the sides of an insect's body through which air passes into breathing tubes.

talon
A hooked claw, e.g. on a bird of prey.

territory
An area that an animal uses for feeding or breeding. Animals defend their territories against others of the same species.

thorax
The middle section of an insect's body. The insect's wings and legs are attached to the thorax.

trachea
The windpipe running from the nose and mouth to transport air to the lungs.

vertebrate
Any animal that has a backbone, e.g. birds, mammals, and reptiles.

warm-blooded
An animal that maintains its body temperature at the same level all the time.

womb
An organ in the body of female mammals in which young grow and are nourished until birth.

Index

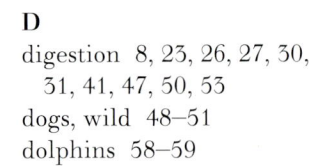

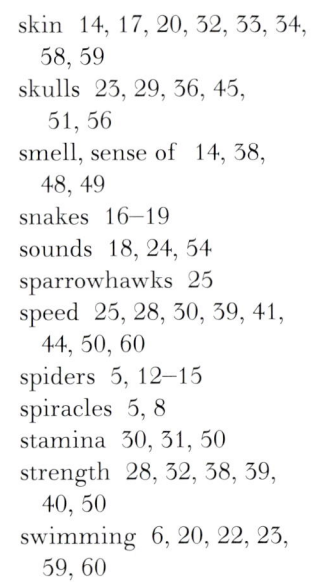

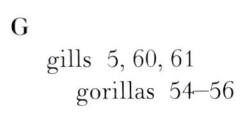